Tucson Justice

by

Mike Stotter

Dales Large Print Books
Long Preston, North Yorkshire,
BD23 4ND, England.

British Library Cataloguing in Publication Data.

Stotter, Mike
    Tucson justice.

    A catalogue record of this book is
    available from the British Library

    ISBN   978-1-84262-786-0 pbk

First published in Great Britain in 1994 by Robert Hale Limited

Copyright © Mike Stotter 1994

Cover illustration © Gordon Crabb by arrangement with
Alison Eldred

The right of Mike Stotter to be identified as the author of this
work has been asserted by him in accordance with the
Copyright, Designs and Patents Act, 1988

Published in Large Print 2010 by arrangement with
Mike Stotter

Dales Large Print is an imprint of Library Magna Books Ltd.

Printed and bound in Great Britain by
T.J. (International) Ltd., Cornwall, PL28 8RW

Here's to the explorers of that far-off continent ... the Bridges. Lesley, Andy, Jamie and Ben.

Far away but never far from my thoughts.

ONE

Jim Brandon stared ahead along the dusty road that led its rutted course to the railhead town that was dimly visible in the heat-haze. He turned in the saddle and said to his companion, 'I've a feeling that we're in for some good fortune here, Joe.'

Reverend Joshua Slate smiled, the amusement touching the corners of his eyes. 'I hope so,' he replied. 'For the past few days you've been itching to get into a card game. You've been crotchety with me playing just for matchsticks. Even *I'll* be glad to see you at a table.'

'I bet you would. 'Sides, the extra cash'll come in handy,' Brandon said, wanting to justify his need to play a hand or two of poker. 'You know we ain't exactly strapped for cash at present, and a good game'll feed our coffers.'

'Sure,' Slate grinned. 'But don't go expecting too much in this little place. Seems to be a developing rail town, though.'

They had reached the twin tracks that cut across the terrain. The sounds of work reached their ears; the clanging of metal and the hiss of steam from a nearby locomotive engine testing its system; the shouting and yelling coming from the railyard, and the occasional bellowing from a handful of beef that were held in a small pen.

They crossed over the tracks to enter the town proper where clapboard buildings lined both sides of a single street, weather-beaten structures of wood and logs that sweltered in the hot sunlight. Passersby dressed in dust covered range clothes gave them a casual glance, a nod of the head, then wordlessly moved on. Slate smiled at the town folk in return whilst Brandon viewed everyone with a cold-eyed impassiveness. They rode towards a building that boasted it was Crane's Mercantile; a two storey wood structured affair, painted in red that assaulted the eye. A sorry-looking roan and a quarter-horse were standing by the hitch-rail, their reins wrapped loosely around the horn of the saddles.

Slate quietly studied the horses, then glanced at Brandon. The gambler caught the meaning of Slate's glance and silently nodded. During their brief spell together as companions, Brandon knew to trust the older man's intuition on matters that were beyond his knowledge. He had no strange feelings about the two horses, they didn't seem out of place in a town like this but if the reverend was taking the time to notice them, then maybe...

Reverend Slate gently pulled back on the lines and brought the wagon to a halt, waited for the mule to settle, then said to Brandon, 'Whoever rides them horses must have a lot of faith in them.'

'I doubt if anybody would want to steal 'em, considering the state they're in,' Brandon replied easily.

A young man, maybe no older than nineteen, stood on the plank walk, pacing up and down. His face was pox-marked with angry red spots vivid against the fish-belly white of his skin and he stood no taller than five-seven with his skeletal frame dressed in tatty range clothes. His long black hair that reached his collar was matted, unwashed and lice-infested. He wore a gunbelt strapped around his waist which looked out of place on him, and he absently toyed with the big belt buckle. He cast a nervous glance with his big brown eyes over at Brandon and Slate and drew in a deep breath.

Slate kept a watchful eye on him as he spoke to Brandon. 'You go and find your game, and I'll freshen up on supplies. No doubt it won't be hard for me to find you.'

Brandon laughed, the feeling of apprehension diminishing with Slate's reassuring words. 'OK, Joe. See you later.' He angled the big grey across the hard-packed street, pausing to look back over his shoulder, but took care not to glance at the youth on the walk. Slate had made no move to get down from his wagon and the claybank that was tied to the rear pawed restlessly at the ground whilst the mule stood passively in the traces.

From inside Crane's Mercantile came a shout, indistinct yet menacing. It was followed by a clearer, angrier voice, calling for help. Then the roar of a gun shattered the morning air like the crack of a bullwhip. Brandon had not yet reached the saloon, and he jerked the grey to an urgent halt and swung around in the saddle.

He watched as the store door burst open and a masked man stumbled out, a still-smoking revolver in one hand and a gunny sack in the other. There was no need to be told twice what was occurring, and he looked over to Slate. The reverend sat rigid in the box seat with his hands held casually in his lap. Brandon knew that the innocent looking preacher was already calculating the chances of making a grab for the Winchester from its hiding place.

Now the youth on the walk jumped down

and grabbed for the reins from the roan and got them unfastened. He was reaching for the other set to the quarter horse when a bullet thudded into the hitch-rail upright, showering him with splinters. He whirled around to his attacker.

'Let them horses be!' ordered a man, stepping off the plank walk from the opposite side of the street, smoke curling from the muzzle of his Winchester rifle.

The youth's face was sheened in sweat, his eyes betrayed his indecision.

'Go to hell, Sheriff!' the man with the neckerchief covering his lower face shouted, raising his pistol.

It was a foolish move on his part, but he wasn't in the frame of mind to think straight. The sheriff raised the rifle to his shoulder and fired again. The would-be robber gasped as the bullet thwacked into his body, knocking him off his feet and setting him down in a sitting position on the walk.

The two horses at the hitch-rail kicked and snorted. The roan whirled around, ripping the reins out of the youth's hand and went galloping down the street, and there was nothing he could do to stop the quarter horse from following. Now he was left exposed and made for an easy target.

'Listen, son,' Slate's voice was deep and calming. 'Don't even think about drawing on the sheriff. It'll go easy on you if you kept that iron in its holster.'

The boy looked up at Slate, a sadness touching his eyes and said, 'Everything ain't always easy, preacher.' Then snatched for the revolver on his hip.

'Damn it, kid!' Slate shouted, raising himself out of the seat.

'You fool!' the sheriff countered, calmly levered the Winchester and shot the youth high in the chest.

The crack of the rifle cut above all other sounds, and the youngster reeled back as blood spurted out of his chest. He bounced off the wall and sprawled face down on the walk. The pistol remained untouched in its holster.

The gun of the masked man sounded as the higher report of the rifle was still echoing over the street. A bullet thudded into the sheriff's leg, and the stout man gave a grunt of surprise, and staggered back but somehow managed to remain on his feet. The sheriff gritted his teeth and worked the Winchester's lever, then snapped off a shot, diving for cover immediately afterwards.

His shot missed the outlaw and the smile that had formed on the sheriff's face now slipped, an angry expression took its place. Surprisingly quick for a man of his size, he leapt up on to his feet, raising the rifle and taking careful aim at the masked outlaw. The rifle barked again. The gun flew from the outlaw's hand as a second bullet hit his body, pushing him down. It wasn't a killing shot, but good enough to keep him from firing the handgun again.

The sheriff reluctantly lowered the rifle, seemingly sorry that there was no one else to shoot at. Only then did he look down at his wound. Blood was spreading across his pants' leg where the bullet had lodged itself in the fleshy part of the thigh. He stood waiting, the rifle held athwart his body.

'There was no need to kill the kid, sheriff,' Slate demanded. 'He wouldn't have pulled that iron.'

'You know that for a fact?'

'I know people, it's part of my job. He wouldn't have done it.'

'Perhaps not, but I weren't prepared to take the chance. Who are you anyhow?'

'Reverend Joshua Slate,' he replied. 'Just a visitor to this little town.'

'I'm Jack Bell, sheriff of Flower Creek.'

'Mmm – if witnesses are needed, sheriff,' Slate said thoughtfully. 'I'll vouch for you…'

'That's mighty white of you.'

'And so will my partner.' Slate nodded to Brandon.

The gambler had dismounted and was leading his grey by the reins, a faint smile played on his lips. Sheriff Bell turned and nodded toward the man. He calmly watched as a crowd began to gather around the two bodies sprawled out on the walk. The attempted robbery of the local mercantile was not what he would consider a success for the men who tried it. He felt euphoric at his dealing with two armed men and began to hum. Acting tough in front of the strangers, but overdoing it.

'Hey, sheriff!' a man from the crowd called out. 'This one's still breathing!'

He turned and looked at the man, his light blue eyes blazing with anger. He walked across the street to where a suited man wearing a brown derby perched atop his head, knelt alongside the downed older outlaw. Out of the corner of his eye, Bell saw both Brandon and Slate had followed him. He did his best to ignore them as he bent down to examine the wounded man. He pulled the neckerchief from the man's face and raised an eyebrow in surprise.

'You know him?' asked Slate, watching the sheriff.

'It ain't no business of yours, but yeah, he's known to me. His name is Butler, runs a hauling business 'tween here and Tucson.' He sighed and ran a hand over his face, his brow creased in puzzlement. 'Hey, Butler! What in God's name d'you think you were doing?'

The outlaw named Butler cracked open his eyes and squinted at the big man. A weak smile crossed his lips. 'Hi, Jack. Things didn't work out as well...' A coughing spasm shook his body, blood bubbling at the corners of his mouth. 'Still, could've been worse ... is Stuart kilt?'

Sheriff Bell nodded his head and Butler closed his eyes and slowly shook his head. 'Damn fool kid,' he whispered. 'I warned him – weren't his job to...' another spasm halted the words.

The sheriff's gaze roved over the man, noted the dark eyes and thin face; the white scar tissues bright against his darker, weather-beaten skin. He still wore the same set of buckskins that Bell had seen him in the day they had first met some six or seven years ago. He was impatient for Butler to carry on. 'What else? You got more to say?'

he demanded.

Butler opened his eyes once again, he looked around at Slate. 'You a preacher?' he asked softly.

'Yes,' answered Slate.

'What denomination?'

Slate sighed. 'Does it matter?'

Butler chuckled, 'Guess not. You mind if I tell you something?'

'Not if you don't mind everyone else listening in,' Slate said with a smile.

'Uh? Get them vultures outta here, Bell.'

'Don't order me around, Butler,' snorted the sheriff. He nodded to the crowd, but his eyes were fixed on Slate. 'OK, get outta here, this ain't no sideshow.' He made it sound like a warning to Slate, coming on tough again, but the preacher couldn't decide whether or not to take him serious so stood his ground.

The crowd grumbled as they were denied seeing the hauler's death and began to drift away. Some stood near Clinton's dead body, morbidly looking at the bullet wounds, the drying blood, the boy's sightless eyes and listening to the drone of gathering flies. Others took up a position on the opposite side of the street, craning their necks to see Butler and the trio surrounding him. Perhaps even to see Butler die. More people were emerging from the saloon with drinks in their hands, nodding and smiling at the spectacle.

Brandon addressed Bell for the first time, 'I think you ought to get him to a doc. Seems as though he might pull through.'

Bell shot him an angry stare. 'Don't tell me my job, mister. I don't like strangers putting their noses into my business.'

'You're scaring me, sheriff,' Brandon said dryly. 'Anyhow, you'd best get him seen to before he leaks all his blood on to the walk.'

'You talk too much,' Bell told him.

In that instant the gambler and the sheriff locked stares. It was a clash of strong wills, and Slate knew who would come out the better. Bell stretched himself up to his full height and turned away, gingerly stepping off the walk and into the street. He waved to one of the crowd and told him to fetch the doc. He turned back and studied the two men.

The younger one was around five feet ten, dark haired and moustachioed. He carried his weight well and his eyes were constantly alert. A single-holster gunbelt was slung around his hips but didn't look natural. He moved kind of awkwardly – not used to its weight. The grey suit with its off-white shirt and black string tie gave his profession away in an instant but it didn't faze Bell in the least.

His companion, the reverend, was not an easy man to sum up in one meeting. He was heavily bearded and his age was difficult to put a year on. He was dressed in traditional black broadcloth, with a grubby white collar at his throat. His hair was the colour of dirty straw and blue eyes were in stark contrast to his sombre dress. Although he carried no visible weapon, Bell was certain that he could make a dangerous enemy. Slate carried that kind of aura.

Bell kicked at the dusty ground as he

waited for the doc to appear, watching as Brandon and Slate fussed around Butler tending to the dying man's needs. He knew that the hauler was going to die when he saw that his bullets had hit close to the man's heart. He didn't want to see the man die, they had shared many a beer and tall story together but by the same token he wouldn't shed any tears at his passing.

The doc appeared out of the saloon and glanced around. He managed to put on an act of having been attending to a patient, as if anyone would have believed him anyhow. He spotted the sheriff and angled across the street with purposeful strides. Coming up to Bell, he went to open his mouth but was stopped by the sheriff's stern expression and the jerk of his thumb indicated the trio, showing where he was needed.

'Keep back! Give him some air!' the doctor ordered officiously, pushing his slight body between Brandon and Slate. He looked down at Butler and tutted.

'So much blood from two little wounds,'

he said.

'They may be little, doc,' Butler grunted. 'But they sure as hell hurt … beggin' your pardon, reverend.'

Slate smiled. 'Don't worry about it.' He looked up at Brandon. His expression was of the 'what the hell can we do about it?' variety.

The doctor grunted as he got up, brushing off the dust from his knees. 'You men get a grip on this feller and tote him over to the station.' He looked over to Bell and said in a louder voice, 'I can't help him here, sheriff. You got to get him to the hospital in Tucson.'

'I haven't the manpower to escort a prisoner, doc. Can't you see to him here?'

The doctor shook his head. 'He needs to be operated on, and I haven't the facilities here. You need your leg seen to as well.' He pointed at the spreading dark stain.

Bell looked down at his wound and said, 'It don't hurt me none. Let's get something done about this jasper!'

Slate stood up and said, 'I'd be prepared to see this man arrives safely in Tucson, sheriff.'

Bell studied Slate, his eyes cold and flat, then glanced at Brandon. 'Why in the hell should I trust you two? You both rode in together when these here gents were pulling off a robbery. Perhaps you're in cahoots with them.'

Slate snorted and virtually jumped down off the walk, took three long-legged strides, and stopped in front of the sheriff. His voice was low, menacing, 'Sometimes it's better to shut your mouth before your brains get into action. You may be quick on the trigger but you're a bit slow up top. I'm a man of the cloth not a common robber – don't make a mistake between the two.' His face was flushed red with anger by the time he finished the sentence.

The spectators were enjoying the confrontation between the men, jostling each other for a better position, hoping that they might even have the chance to see the gunplay they had already missed. The tension that spread itself across Flower Creek's main street was almost tangible. An onlooker cleared his throat loudly and was almost set upon by fellow spectators.

Bell could feel the countless eyes on him, and nodded towards Butler. 'Taking him to Tucson will mean the county'll pay you deputy rates...'

'Don't insult me by offering blood money,' Slate snarled. 'I'll take him because it's part of my duties to do so. There's such a thing called humanity, and I reckon that you were at the back of the queue when they were dishing it out.'

'Don't preach to me about humanity!' Bell was indignant at Slate's accusation. 'These are hard times! With men who'd rather blow your head off than give you a howdy! You want to sit on this side of a star and see what crap you get dealt before you get all sancti-monious, *reverend*.'

Slate knew that Bell was right, a sheriff's job wasn't all tax collecting and socialising. There was always that unknown element – a darkened alley hiding a vengeful brother or a belligerent drunkard ready to pump lead in your direction. But on the other hand, he was being paid for a job, and if he didn't like it, Bell could always unpin the badge, saddle up and leave. Simple as that. But Slate had seen the man in action, saw the blood-lust in his eyes as he calmly shot down the two outlaws. He remembered the look of dis-appointment on the man's face when there was no one else left to kill. Bell was a bad-ass, and he knew it. Slate acknowledged that a man like Sheriff Bell would sooner die than give up that 50c tin star on his vest.

'I allow you that, sheriff,' Slate admitted. 'But as a man of God I must look after my fellow man, and that includes injured robbers. So, what's it to be?'

Sheriff Bell answered without hesitation, 'Aw, damn'! Take Butler and get the hell outta here!' Dismissing the preacher with a casual wave of his hand.

Bell was left standing in the dusty street, a look of defeat on his face. He watched as the three men lifted Butler into the reverend's wagon and set off toward the station. He knew that this should be his business but he remained silent as he watched the men ride down the street and thought that a telegram to the sheriff's office in Tucson would suffice.

Sighing, he turned and saw that the gunnysack filled with money still lay on the floor. He stepped up on to the plank walk and picked it up. 'Christ! Charlie Crane!' he said out loud. 'I'd clean forgot about him.' Then ventured into the store to find Crane's corpulent body crumpled across his counter. The *drip-dripping* of blood pattered into a glaireous pool on the floor. Butler had blown most of Crane's head away in the robbery – not a difficult shot from only two feet away. A vile taste rose in Bell's mouth and he swallowed hard, and for the first time he could feel pain in his leg. He turned his back on the dead man and limped out of the store, leaving a trail of his own blood in his tread. Then, felt all of his thirty-five years weighing down on his shoulders when he realised that he would have to tell Jessica Crane of her husband's demise.

TWO

Brandon hauled himself up into the baggage car and reached out and took the dying man by the armpits. 'Take care, Joe,' he said.

Slate held on to Butler's legs and let Brandon take most of the man's weight before swinging the lower half of the body on to the straw. The hauler groaned as he was lowered to the floor, a bolt of pain racking his upper body.

He knew there wasn't a chance in hell of surviving the journey to the hospital, it was a trip of more than fifty miles, and he was just holding on to consciousness. He shut his eyes to the pain and watched the swirls of coloured flashes play across his eyelids. He should have been grateful to these two men trying to save his life because if it had been left to Sheriff Bell, he'd still be laid out on the planking outside the store, blood staining the wood a dirty brown. The reverend said that he would see that he would get him to Tucson, one way or the other, and he believed him.

Butler opened his eyes and saw the younger man get out of the car and walk towards the horses. The reverend bunched up handfuls of straw, pushed them under the man's head, then sat back.

His voice was soothing when he spoke, 'We'll soon be on our way and get you to hospital. They'll take good care of you there.'

'You know I ain't gonna make it, reverend.'

'Hey, have a bit of faith, will you?' said Slate. 'It's not a long trip; you're a tough hombre, you'll last out till we get you there.'

Butler shook his head, 'Huh-uh. I know I ain't gonna survive this trip. That bastard Bell made sure of that!'

Slate knew the man was right but said, 'You got to be more positive, Butler. A man ain't dead until he's breathed his last.'

'That in the Bible?'

Slate shook his head. 'Not that I know of, but it's a fact.'

Butler swallowed hard. 'I ain't… I know I ain't been a practising Catholic for some time, but would you listen to my confession?'

'I'm not a priest.'

'I've got to tell it, though. Will you listen?'

Slate nodded.

By the time Brandon brought their saddle-bags to the baggage car, the aged hauler had lapsed into unconsciousness. He glanced down at Butler, the man was breathing shallowly, and the amount of blood staining his buckskins indicated that it didn't look good for him.

Brandon looked at Slate.

'Well?' he said.

Slate looked back at him, shaking his head. 'It doesn't look good, Jim.'

Brandon snorted. 'Looks like we've ended up with a dead man, then.'

Slate run a hand through his beard and said wearily, 'Yeah, it does. The last thing we can do for him is to make sure he gets a decent burial.'

'Yep, but I'm sure his local sky pilot'll see to that, eh?'

Slate coughed, then said, 'Well ... he asked me to look after matters. A private ceremony; just his wife and us.'

'Us?'

'That's the way he wanted it, Jim.'

Brandon shook his head. 'I ... we ... don't even know the man.'

Slate looked a little stunned. 'Jim, you got to respect a dyin' man's wishes. He told me he didn't have many friends in Tucson and seeing we were kind enough to look after him...'

'OK, I get it.' Brandon sat down heavily in the straw, took off his hat and scratched vigorously at his crown. Feeling much better for that he replaced the hat on top his head and brought out a pack of cards and began a game of solitaire.

The Baldwin pulled into the town of Tucson amidst the high-pitched squeal of brakes and great clouds of billowing white steam. The train settled to a halt; carriage doors were flung open, passengers alighted and workers of the Southern Pacific Rail Road hustled across the platform with their trolleys aiding females and the more affluent looking gentlemen.

Further down the train a guard opened the door to the baggage car and stepped back sharply as the foul odour hit him in the face.

'Jesus Christ! What you got in there, a dead polecat?'

Slate stood up, towering over the man. 'Not quite, my son. A dead man.'

The guard's mouth dropped open as he became aware of his blasphemy and his face reddened. 'I'm ... I'm sorry, reverend. I didn't know.'

'How could you?' Slate said sharply. 'Now I'd like you to get a litter for the deceased and a message to the sheriff.'

'Sure, sure.' The guard stuttered, turned sharply on his heels and all but broke into a run.

Brandon and Slate watched the over-weight porter waddle down the platform. The gambler said, 'You sure put the fear of God into him, Joe.'

'Well, someone's got to do the job.'

'I've watched you, you know? You like putting people on the spot with your Holier-than-thou attitude. You wrong foot 'em and make 'em feel small.'

'Do I?'

'Yeah, you did it to Bell back there, now you cut that guard down to size.'

'I hadn't noticed,' said Slate.

'I suppose you've been doing it so long, you wouldn't have done.'

Slate shrugged. 'You could be right.' He lowered himself out of the car and down on to the wooden platform saying, 'But I'm too long in the tooth to change my ways now.'

Yes, you are, Brandon thought, *but you are a wily sonofagun as well.* During the train ride to town, Brandon had watched Slate surreptitiously as he idly played his game of solitaire. The older, ex-cavalryman had been deep in thought, staring at the caboose wall in front of him, eyes unfocused. Brandon could only guess that the hauler had said something to him which may have sent him into this deep reverie. He came out of it when Butler breathed a last, rattling breath and slipped away.

They both knew that it was inevitable that the man would die, and Slate gave a heavy sigh as he made a sign of the cross. He began to say a prayer for the dead man. His voice was full of emotion which surprised Brandon, they hadn't known the man yet Slate's words were meaningful. Poignant.

Now Brandon felt that their work was done. They had kept their promise to Sheriff Bell, and it was up to the law to take care of matters from hereon in. He said to Slate, 'Joe, our work's done. I'm going to see if I can get us booked in some place.'

'Yeah, sure. I'll meet you at the hospital, I'd like to see that they take care of him.'

Brandon was puzzled. 'Why all the concern, Joe?'

'Have you ever been alone?' Slate asked. 'So alone it makes you want to cry?'

'No, but…'

'A man's soul can be left wandering alone in this world, Jim. That's why there's so many troubled spirits around.'

Brandon looked at Slate, thinking the man was joking with him, but one look into those fierce blue eyes he knew Slate was serious. So Brandon didn't smile, no laugh escaped his lips, he nodded gravely and touched the brim of his hat to Butler, then walked slowly down the platform.

The man banged his fist on the table, the noise enough to silence the excited small-talk that filled the room. All heads turned to look at him, and he swept his eyes across the sea of familiar faces. The room fell into a hushed silence and they waited for him to speak.

'What I got to say ain't good,' he began. 'It seems that our lawyers have failed in the federal court to have our case heard.'

There was an immediate uproar: a mixture of defeated moans and defiant shouts. The man raised his hand for silence, waited, then continued. 'As the spokesman of the Settlers' League, I have tried various ways to get the railroad to recognise our legal claims, but every which way we turn we are thwarted by them. We sent our contracts to Congress, they turned them down; we sent our own lawyers to court, and we were turned out, again.'

'What we gonna do?' pleaded a voice from the back.

'You are fully aware that I do not advocate violence, but the time has come to make sure that the land we have developed from an arid place to a fertile paradise be made safe for our sons and daughters.

'Already the Johanssons have been forced out of their homes and strangers have moved in, tapping into our irrigation canals, diverting the water for their own use. I vote that we oust those people bodily and see to it that no one can take their place!'

Shouts of agreements filled the room.

Men raised their clenched fists in the air and angrily shook them around. The man at the table, Henri Jacques, a third generation Frenchman, smiled encouragingly at his fellow settlers. He knew the kind of anger he was inciting, but it made no impression on his feelings. He had toiled his land for more than five years under an agreement with the railroad that should have allowed him to buy his land at the rate of $3.00 an acre when developed, but the League had discovered that their farms were being placed on the open market at anywhere between $25 to $40 an acre. Anyone with the money could purchase whichever farm they wanted so long as they had the money.

If the railroad wanted a fight, then by God, he would give them one.

He held his hands up for silence, then said, 'All of those who are with me, meet me in one hour's time outside my home. Bring no guns, I'll not use them in our fight, and there will be no argument on this.' Jacques looked around the room, searching for a face. Finding the tall and well-dressed Englishman half-way down the room, his spectacles reflecting the coal-oil lamps' light, said, 'Ken Pemberton, you'll bring your flatbed and two barrels of oil.'

This was met with a murmur of excited voices.

Jacques went on, 'One hour's time, gentlemen. We shall see what the Southern Rail Road Company is made of.'

For some that hour could not go fast enough. The light had gone out of the sky and a star-specked canopy greeted them as they gathered out front of Jacques' farmhouse. All were on horseback, except for Ken Pemberton who sat on the flatbed with its two barrels of oil safely lashed to the sides. They spoke amongst themselves in low, conspiratorial tones. Spoke of their defiance to the big railroad company and how they were going to get even. The farmhouse door opened and a hush fell over them.

Jacques stood in the doorway, backlit by an oil lamp set on a table, his voice strong and in command when he spoke, 'Tonight, we strike the first blow for the Settlers' League. We will take back the Johansson farm from those who do not rightly own it. No harm will befall them, however, they are not to blame. Now men, we ride!'

Henri Jacques headed the column of riders stiff-backed and without fear. He was a small man who carried his sparse frame well; dark, brooding brown eyes surveyed the land around him and his calloused and liver-spotted hands gripped the reins with calm authority. Jacques had told his wife of the League's decision and she simply nodded her assent. His three young daughters were safely tucked up in their bed, unaware of how the events going on around them would affect their future.

It was their future that Jacques was fighting to protect. Theirs and hundreds, perhaps thousands like them. If he were to bow to the railroad now, who was to say that others like the Swedish-born Johanssons wouldn't have their homes and land taken away from them?

This defiant stance the Settlers' League was taking could be the first among many to protect any settler and family, and his decision not to use weapons might be of importance later on.

He glanced over his shoulder, looking back over the riders, and as far as he could tell no one had brought either shotguns or revolvers, he smiled as he shifted the length of brush-wrapped hickory stick from one hand to another.

Within the hour they were on the land which now belonged to John Taylor, formerly the Johanssons' acreage. A single light showed at the farmhouse window and Jacques pushed the Morgan towards it. The riders reached the farmyard, spreading out in a long line with each man remaining in the saddle. Jacques halted his horse and called out, 'John Taylor! Come to the door!'

He could hear surprised voices coming from inside the house, then a chair falling backward, crashing down on the bare floorboards.

He called again, 'John Taylor! This is Henri Jacques, I have the men of the Settlers' League with me. We are not armed, please come to the door.'

He waited for the tranchea to be slid back, nervously biting the inside of his bottom lip, holding his breath. Finally the door opened enough for John Taylor to slip out, pulling the door quickly closed behind him.

'What is it? What do you want?' he demanded.

'We mean you no harm, Taylor,' Jacques said, 'but our hand has been forced by the railroad.'

'What are you talkin' about, mister?'

'Get your family outside, Taylor.' Jacques' tone became tinged with harshness. 'This is not your home...'

'It damn' well is!'

'You bought your property under a false pretence. The Johanssons are the rightful owners, but you dispossessed them and we mean to dispossess you.'

'I don't know what you're talkin' about,

but no one is going to throw me out of my home!'

Jacques shifted uneasily in the saddle. 'Don't make things any harder,' he pleaded. 'Bring out your family, that's all.'

'Over my dead body!'

This was what Jacques had been afraid of; the man was rightly outraged but he had to be removed. He called on three of the League members to restrain John Taylor, which they did swiftly and without harm. He then dismounted and signalled for others to follow him into the house.

Within five minutes they had removed Taylor's family and their meagre possessions, then used the oil from Pemberton's flatbed to soak the house. Jacques could not look at the Taylors as he ignited his torch and set the house aflame.

THREE

Heber Carson sat opposite his partner, Perry Willard, and finished the last bite of his breakfast, using a slice of bread to mop up the mess of egg yolk and bacon fat, then said, 'Tell me that bit again.'

'What part?'

'You know, the bit when we get to use the sheriff.'

Willard sighed. It wasn't that his partner was slow on the uptake, it was just that Carson liked to hear the part of their plan where they worked alongside a sheriff instead of running from him. So he told him, again.

Carson smiled a lazy grin and looked around the room. He caught his reflection in one of the sparkling mirrors surrounding them and liked what he saw: a young man just turned twenty-six, slicked-back black hair and a thick, drooping moustache. His squinting eyes took in his shabby clothes shrouding his heavy-set frame and smirked. He let his appearance fool others into thinking he was a Goddamned simpleton. He turned back to Willard.

Carson said, 'You sure you got the papers?'

'How many times have I got to check?'

'We don't want to make mistakes, do we?'

Willard slowly shook his head and put his hand into his inside pocket, pulled out a batch of papers tied with a red ribbon and waved them under Carson's nose.

'There,' he said, 'satisfied now?'

'Yeh,' Carson said.

The men lapsed into silence as they waited for the waiter to remove their emptied plates, and ordered two glasses of their finest cognac, ignoring the spiteful looks they were receiving from other patrons of the Xan Xavier Hotel in Tucson. Perry Willard shifted in his seat, anxious to get their business started as quickly as possible.

'I'm gonna see what's taking him so long,'

Willard said.

'Hey, Perry. Take it easy, will you?' Carson said easing towards his partner. 'Don't want to draw attention to ourselves, eh?'

'Suppose you're right,' Willard nodded. 'I'm eager to be out of here, pronto. This place makes me feel uncomfortable.'

Carson agreed and sat back. He was a patient man; it was one of his main strengths, that and his usefulness with a handgun. He wasn't lightning fast but he could hit what he mostly aimed at, and that meant something. He had been working with Willard for the past year, hiring themselves out to the big men who didn't want to soil their hands on the dirty jobs they'd sooner pay to have done. If others wanted to turn away an easy dollar by frightening nesters or take a hand in the odd woolly war, then that was okay by him. Meant there was more greenbacks for him and Willard to pick up.

He had laughed when the businessman approached them with the latest deal. Laughed until he heard how much was being put down up front. Now they had travelled first class to Tucson and their rooms were the best the hotel had to offer, all paid for and part of the deal. It was easy money, especially when they were being backed by the sheriff. The thought made him smile.

'What're you grinning at?' asked Willard.

'Oh, just thinking 'bout the deal.'

'Yeah, still seems crazy, don't it?'

'Won't be too long before we pick up the other two grand,' said Carson.

'Yeah, an' I'm waitin' to see his dumbstruck face when we turn up on his porch.'

'That'll be a sight, for sure.'

Heber Carson looked up and saw the sheriff walk into the restaurant over the rim of his brandy balloon. It was his third and its effects were beginning to tell on him. He made eye contact with the man and signalled him over.

Sheriff Pete Breen made his way between the tables, smiling and raising his hat to familiar faces, saying a warm 'good morning'. Then, without being asked, he pulled out a chair to sit down opposite Carson and Will-

ard. He didn't launch into any formal intro-
ductions and said, 'A cable came through this
morning. 'Pears that our friend has over-
stepped his mark. I'm to go with you out to
his spread and that of one other, and do
what's necessary. I take it you gents are
ready?'

Willard nodded.

'Good. I hope that you brought your ... er
... equipment with you?'

'Never far from our sides, sheriff,' Carson
slurred, patting the clumsy looking Smith &
Wesson Frontier 44-40.

Breen shot him a sideways glance. 'You in
a fit state to start out right now?'

'Yeh.'

'I mean ... you haven't had one of those too
many?' he said pointing to the brandy glass.

Carson shook his head. 'Won't affect my
aim none if that's what you're talkin' about,
sheriff.'

'Hey! There's to be no shootin', remember?'

Carson leaned across the table and locked

stares with Breen and said in a low, menacing his, 'I don't tell you your job – you don't tell me mine.'

Oh, shit, Breen thought, *they've sent me a mad dog killer.* 'Listen to me,' he said. 'You know the deal, eh? Keep to it and you'll be both rich men by the end of the day.'

Carson belched loudly, ignoring the stares from surrounding diners and got to his feet.

'Perry, see to the horses,' he said. 'I'll fetch our equipment. I'll meet you out front.'

Breen watched Carson weave an unsteady path between the tables, occasionally knocking purposefully into a patron, then took the stairs to the first floor. Breen turned to Willard and said, 'Look, don't get me wrong, but are you sure of him?'

Willard's hard blue eyes looked back at Breen. 'He's only play actin', sheriff,' he said. 'Got this thing about makin' people uneasy around him. Kinda makes him feel dangerous, you know what I mean?'

Pete Breen blinked nervously, 'Yeah, sort of.'

Willard lifted a fat Havana cigar from his top pocket and bit the end off, then used a lucifer to light it. He blew out a cloud of blue smoke and leaned closer to Breen, saying, 'I blame it on Billy Bonney, you know.'

'How's that?'

'Well, Heb's got a thing 'bout the kid. Idolises him in a way. Folks say that when Bonney was around he kept people on their toes, they couldn't tell what way he would jump. One minute he was a good natured boy, the next *bam!*, you're dead.'

Breen shook his head knowing his first summing up of the man named Carson was right. Why did folks idolise the wrong people? he thought. What was wrong in being like Lincoln, Bridger or Frémont? You try and stop a six year old to ask who they were and what would he say? 'Who?' Even when John Frémont himself was living in a rented house right here in town. Seems that every yonkster wanted to be an outlaw: playing street games with wooden toy guns; shoot 'em ups and robbers. Christ!

Hopefully those days were coming to an end now that the Southern Pacific had arrived in Tucson. The town had electric lights and a new telephone system, and he had heard the mayor had recently applied for the town to be incorporated as a city; there was even talk of a university being built, but all that remained in the future. What he had to deal with first was the present and he watched Willard stand up.

He was surprised that the man was small. He didn't know why but he expected him to be tall, perhaps it was because the man's upper frame looked compact. His close-cut dark hair had been neatly pomaded and a heavy moustache cut across his top lip and hung down his wide-boned face.

Willard said, 'Finished?'

'Uh?'

'I ain't no prize bull.'

'Hey, I'm sorry. I didn't realise…'

'OK, don't worry,' Willard replied casually.

Breen was pleased that Willard was an easygoing man, and nothing like his partner.

'I think we'd better go,' Willard said, 'Heb's gonna be waiting.'

Breen laid a hand on Willard's forearm, his face serious when he said, 'I don't mean to be insulting, but your partner...'

'What about him?'

'He's not likely to go in guns blazing is he?'

Willard said, 'Sheriff, one thing I never do is vouch for my partner's actions. He'll do whatever he wants to do and there ain't nothing short of a Sharps' .50 can stop him doing it.'

It wasn't the answer that Breen wanted to hear but was thankful that Willard was being truthful. The sheriff hitched up his pants and straightened his jacket.

He said, 'I guess we'll have to play this thing by ear.' Then started out of the restaurant without waiting for Willard.

FOUR

Joshua Slate had spent the best part of the previous night talking with the priest from Our Lady's church in the hospital chapel. The place was basic: three rows of hardback chairs on either side of the aisle faced a cloth covered altar on which stood two silver candlesticks, and a simple cross hung on the wall behind. The remaining adobe walls were unadorned. The room was cold. So cold their breath showed misty white on the air when they spoke.

The man known only as Butler had been cleaned up by attendants who had laid him out on a table, and covered him with a clean white cloth pulled up to his chin. Even in death there was nothing to hide the man's weariness. Slate suppressed the feeling of sadness welling up inside of him and turned

51

his eyes away from the basic wooden cross, and settled on the thin-faced man opposite him.

Father Caleb Weller sat languidly in a chair and listened to the story concerning Butler's demise. His vocation called for him to be a patient listener, and whilst he pushed his wire-framed glasses back up his nose whenever they slipped out of position, he listened and absently rubbed at the bald patch in his much-thinning hair as Slate's deep voice echoed around the otherwise silent chapel.

'You're sure of that?' Weller asked when Slate had finished.

'I'm certain he said that,' replied Slate, leaning forward. 'Why?'

'It's just that, as far as I know, the man was not married.'

Slate fingered his beard. 'I'm certain that he said "my woman"; said they lived just out of town, where the railroad was construct-ing new shops. That mean anything to you?'

'Yes, it sounds right,' Weller allowed. 'I

mean, that's where he lived. And he was working for the railroad on a casual basis, supplying them with goods and the such. But I'm mystified about this talk of a wife, or ... a woman ... as he would call her.' He adjusted his glasses again and sighed. 'To my knowledge, and I've been here since 1873, Butler has never been married. I'm sorry that I cannot be of more help to you there, reverend.'

Slate nodded and stifled a yawn, apologising to Weller. 'Perhaps I'll take a look over that way come morning.'

Weller nodded. 'If you do find anything, please let me know. I try and pride myself on my knowing my flock, but he was a lapsed soul... I don't mean to sound sanctimonious, you understand? His comings and goings were fairly irregular and it became hard to keep up with him. I fear it was my fault, I simply lost contact. Perhaps if I had...'

'No, Father,' Slate said and placed his hand gently on Weller's shoulder. 'There was nothing you could have done.'

'Hmm, perhaps not,' Weller accepted.

'Thank you for your company, Father Weller. I must find my young companion. He was to meet me here, but alas, the sins of Dame Fortune rides him hard.'

Weller smiled weakly. 'Ah, I know, I know.'

The men shook hands and Slate left Weller alone in the chapel, his boots clicking loud across the cold flagged floor. He hadn't realised how badly the corpse had smelt and stepping out into the street took the chance to clear his head by breathing deep of the balmy air.

Jim Brandon hadn't kept his promise to meet him, and the reverend now had the thankless task of entering the various saloons, pool halls and possibly the dance halls to find him. He let out a weary sigh, pulled his jacket collar up and moved off towards the first saloon with its single electric light burning bright outside. The sounds of a tinny piano and loud voices filtered out into the street, fighting against other Tucson nightlife noises.

Suddenly, he felt the need of a beer and more cheery company. For some unknown reason, the hauler's death had gotten under his skin. He didn't have a rational explanation for the emotion, so he was only too glad when he pushed open the saloon door, and the heat and the noise greeted him like an old friend.

Jim Brandon sat at a round table in one corner of the saloon playing five card stud poker with four other men. His hat had been shoved to the back of his head and he traced his forefinger along the line of a recent bullet wound. A welt of scabrous skin marked the bullet's path, showing white where the hair above his temple had been removed and failed to grow again.

His steely eyes looked down at his face-up cards: a pair of tens and the eight of spades. He held the ten of diamonds as his hole card, and he waited silently for the final round of betting to take place. The glass of beer at his elbow had hardly been touched and whilst he waited he calculated who, amongst the players, were the most serious-minded.

He looked across to the player opposite him. The big, cherub-faced guy with a moustache shot through with grey, wore a sheepskin jacket over a hickory shirt, and certainly didn't play as well as he thought he did. To his right, a weasely-looking runt of a man had fidgeted throughout the game, his eyes lighting up like fireworks whenever he was dealt a decent hand. The third player was obviously a businessman with nothing better to do than spend a couple of hours in the company of men of whom his opinion was undisguised. He was dressed formally in a Prince Albert frock coat, a freshly laundered white shirt and string tie. Brandon pegged him as being not only tolerated but treated in an obsequious manner by the others around the table. The fourth player appeared at odds with the rest. Dressed in a brown suit that had seen better days, a frayed collared once-white shirt topped with a bright red neckerchief. He had sat drinking water and hardly a word had passed his lips, except to check or raise. He had opened the betting with five dollars and as the betting increased with each card he never balked at the rising cost although he appeared not to be able to afford it.

The betting fell to Sheepskin, and he cast a glance to Brandon expecting some kind of reaction when he said, 'I'll go with it, an' raise it thirty.'

He didn't get one.

The businessman raised an eyebrow and said, 'Uh, that's me out of it. I fold.'

'Count me out, too,' Weasel said, following the businessman's play as he had done all evening, like a dog following its master.

The businessman smiled. It seemed genuine enough but Brandon saw a harshness lurking behind those dark brown eyes.

'Order up another bottle,' he said to Weasel, 'an' put it on my tab.'

Weasel flashed a yellow-toothed grin and said, 'Sure thing, Mister Gilburn.'

Brandon ignored the trivial small-talk and

addressed himself to the water drinker. 'Raise it ten bucks.' The man didn't take his eyes off of his cards, or even seem to acknowledge Brandon. He waited a moment or two before putting forty dollars into the middle of the table.

'Your forty, plus twenty,' he said to Brandon.

'That's too rich for me,' Sheepskin said and threw his cards onto the discard pile. He sat back in the chair and folded his hands across his ample stomach.

Brandon picked up his beer, took a swig and looked at his cards again. Beer froth clung to his moustache like the dying snows of spring. He casually wiped it away and peeled off six ten dollars bills from the small pile in front of him, dropped them into the middle of the table, the added another two tens. He was enjoying the game now, and felt confident enough that his three tens were better than the water-drinker's pair of nines and the ace of diamonds.

With Sheepskin out of the game it only left

the water drinker and himself, and Brandon had a feeling about him: a man who never hedged his bets. Not once had he bluffed in any of the previous games and when he had won, his cards had always been good. But there still was one more card to be dealt.

Wordlessly, his opponent put down his eighty dollars onto a growing pile, then Sheepskin, as dealer, turned over the final cards: a further nine to the water drinker and the eight of clubs to Brandon. The Kansas gambler knew that he had the beating of the man and put his eighty dollars and raised it by a further fifty.

For the first time, Brandon noticed a hesitance in the other man's game. It was as if he was trying to decide if his hand was better than Brandon's. The only way for him to find out was to equalise the betting. And that's what he did.

Jim Brandon flicked over his hole card and showed his full house. His opponent revealed his card and the best he could do was the three nines.

'I was sure I had you there,' he said to Brandon in a rare moment of friendliness. 'That's the second big pot you've taken tonight.'

Brandon scooped the money from the middle and pulled it in front of him. 'D'you know the old saying?' he asked him.

'No, what's that?'

'"A wise player should accept his throws and score them, not bewail his luck".'

'Who said that?' Sheepskin butted in

'Sophocles,' Brandon replied with a half-smile.

'Who in the hell's that? Some goddamn' Injun chief or something?'

'I believe he was a Greek philosopher.'

The men at the table turned and looked at the new speaker. They saw a tall, bearded, distinguished-looking preacher standing behind Brandon, holding a glass of beer in one hand and a half-eaten pickled egg in the other. Brandon hadn't turned, he recognised the voice straight off.

'Hi, Joe,' he said.

'I figgered to find you at a table,' Slate said. 'I thought we'd arranged to meet.'

'Yeah, I kinda got distracted.'

'So I see.' He took a mouthful of beer, then said, 'I need to talk to you.'

'OK, after...'

'No, now,' Slate insisted.

Brandon pushed his chair back and picked up his money, pushing the thick roll into his pants' pocket. 'Sorry, gents. I'm being called away by a higher power, but no doubt I'll be back.'

The businessman stood up and said, 'We'll be here tomorrow night if you fancy your chances again, mister...'

'Name's Jim Brandon, and you're?'

'Don Gilburn.'

'See you later, then.' He touched the brim of his hat and turned away.

Brandon and Slate moved away from the table and pushed their way toward the bar, steering clear of the small stage where the piano player was resuming his position by the upright. A young-looking girl, dressed in a low-cut bodice that pushed the tops of her breasts together like a brace of ripe squashes, a hooped skirt, pink tights with high-heels appeared from behind the curtains to a chorus of shrill wolf-whistles and excited shouts.

Brandon stopped to take a longer and better look at her but Slate gripped his upper arm and pushed him toward a quieter spot at the bar. He ordered two beers before he began to tell the gambler about his late-night conversation with Father Weller.

'Seems to me,' Brandon said, 'that either Weller's mistaken or Butler had been lyin' to you.'

'Why would he lie?'

Brandon shrugged his shoulders.

Slate said, 'I think that Butler was telling the truth but bending it a little.'

'What? Perhaps he was living with the woman and they weren't married?'

'Something like that.'

'That ain't so much of a sin. D'you think that it would make that much of a difference to us if we knew the truth?'

Slate shook his head. 'I doubt it, but he knew he was dyin', and dyin folk don't tell lies on their death bed.'

'Well, I ain't had much experience in that area so I'll take your word on that.' He gulped his beer, then. 'So, how are we gonna find out the truth?'

'The one thing I've got in mind is to post a notice outside the sheriff's office saying that friends and relatives of Butler are welcome along to the funeral.' He finished his beer and put the glass down on the counter. 'He's being interred tomorrow afternoon, Father Weller said he'll conduct the service. We'll have to wait until then to find out anything. Meantime, there's some visiting to do come morning.'

'Such as?'

'Find that woman Butler claimed to be his wife.'

'But you just said…'

'I'd like to settle a few things in my own mind before the funeral, OK?'

'Er … sure,' came Brandon's hesitant reply. He waved the barkeep over and ordered fresh drinks. His eyes wandered back to the stage area but couldn't see the girl, and her voice wasn't loud enough to cut above the yammering around him. He pulled his attention back to Slate.

'I've enough to get us a room for a couple of nights. And there's a game tomorrow night that could finance the rest of our trips to Yellowstone.'

The following morning did live up to Brandon's expectations. Whilst he and Slate saw to their daily ablutions in an upstairs room of the Xan Xavier Hotel, Heber Carson, Perry Willard and Sheriff Pete Breen stepped off the sidewalk and ambled over to the hitching rail outside the lawman's office. Already the hot August sun was beating down on the hard packed street, bouncing off adobe and wood in furnace waves of heat. The sheriff adjusted his hat to shade his eyes a little better, and stopping by his buggy said to Willard: 'It may be better if you rode alongside me.'

Willard looked at him. 'Any reason as to why I should?'

Breen gestured empty handedly, 'Just that it might appear better when we pull up there.'

Willard couldn't understand the reasoning behind that, and said so. Breen explained: 'They know and trust me, so if they see that you're riding with me, it'll set them at ease. Now, they see two mounted, armed strangers *and* me, they just might become edgy.'

Willard nodded slowly. 'I get your drift, sheriff. That's dandy by me. Heb rides his own mount and I'll stick with you: sounds reasonable.'

Carson toed leather and settled himself in the saddle. He looked down at the two men. 'Let's quit jawing and get movin'. The sooner we do this, the soon as we'll be richer for it.'

Breen was tempted to tell Carson he was a conceited sonofabitch and would have done so but for the fact that Carson would use the .44 on him. So he bit his tongue and stepped up into the Carter buggy, taking a hold of the lines. Willard laid a full-length American Arms shotgun on the floor and clapping his hands together said gleefully, 'OK, sheriff, let's get this show on the road.'

The stench of rotting sheep and vegetable manure wafted in the fetid air. It was emanating from a stack more than four feet high and the same in width. Sheriff Breen guided the buggy around the manure heap, aimed the vehicle across the yard and stopped outside of the main house.

Carson remained mounted on his handsomely-marked Colorado Ranger, his greedy eyes scanning the farm and mentally taking stock of the spread: the neat picket fence, the large, well-tended kitchen garden and the rows of brightly-coloured flowers he didn't know the name of but liked all the same. His right hand had drifted away from the pommel and settled on his right thigh, close to the de-thronged .44. His face was void of any emotion as he continued his unchallenged survey.

Willard was content to remain seated in the buggy. This wasn't to be his spread, he and Carson had agreed that during their train journey into Tucson. His was in another part of the valley, some eight miles to the north of this place. Close enough to remain neighbours, though. He heard noises coming from the house and smiled. He had always enjoyed the comforts of a home life; the sounds of a wife going about her business; babes crying and gurgling; all the reassuring sounds of a busy household.

A home.

A black cloud descended in his mind's eye, blotting out this scene, replacing it with what he once had: a wife, children, a farm and a way of life. Before the War; before the Indian attack that snatched it all from him.

Willard thought that he had put the past behind him; spending more than three years on the vengeance trail. Looting, burning and killing any and all Indians that got in his way.

The ironic thing about it though, was that the government had actually paid him to do it. He had legally killed those men, women and children to satisfy his personal blood lust.

Then, after three long bloody years, he had had enough. He quit working for the government and tried his hand at any job that came along. Finally he settled down on a ranch helping to raise Hereford cattle for an Englishman up in Montana. That lasted until the old man, what was his name now? Harvey? Yeh, that was it, J.B. Harvey, was shot by 'assassins unknown', as the marshal put it. But he knew who killed the English-man and he caught up with the runt and cut the bastard in half with a shotgun. Spilled his guts across the walkway, and spat in Jimmy Sandon's face.

When he had satisfied himself that he had avenged Harvey's death he rode out of Hernesfield with the marshal and his posse snapping at his heels. Yeh that Marshal Jim Muir had been the last of the hard breed all right, Willard remembered. A lawman with

Indian blood running in his veins; tough as old boots and wily as an Apache.

Even when his posse was done in, and he had sent them all back save one, he continued on. He and the half-breed (Willard never knew his name) gave chase for more than a month, and near-as-damn done for him at a river crossing. If it hadn't been for Heb Carson butting in with his .44, Willard knew he would have been a goner. So he and Carson formed their partnership with blood and had been on the run since, with a $1,000 reward on their heads.

As he shifted on the padded seat he could feel a certain amount of sympathy for the family about to be evicted from their home, but at least they would be together. Be able to start a new life somewhere else. Sure, it would be tough but they had each other. What in hell's name did he have?

'I said, are you ready?'

Sheriff Breen was standing on the ground, looking up at him.

Willard shook himself from his rumination and concentrated on the present.

'Yeh, must have been dreamin' 'bout somethin',' he replied absently. 'You got them papers?'

Breen patted his breast pocket. 'All safe and well.'

Willard said, 'Hand 'em over, sheriff.' He held out his hand and Breen reluctantly gave him the papers.

'You ready, Heb?' Willard said to Carson.

'Huh-uh.'

Breen and Willard walked up to the closed farmhouse door, whilst Carson remained mounted. The sheriff rapped hard on the door and waited. The door swung open, and who Willard guessed must have been Mrs Jacques stood in the doorway. She was no taller than Breen, even with her hair swept up into a bun on top of her head. She looked tired, a bone piercing weariness that all farm wives seemed to have but her voice was surprisingly light and cheerful as she welcomed the sheriff, genuinely pleased to see him.

'Pete, how are you?' The smiled wiped

away the tiredness from her eyes and set them sparkling. 'We haven't seen you around for some time. How's your Annie?'

'Fine, Mary, fine. Look, can we talk?'

'Sure thing.' She moved towards him.

Breen said, 'I think we'd better talk inside.'

Mary Jacques was puzzled.

'What's wrong, Pete?' she asked. 'And who are these men?'

'C'mon, Mary, don't worry.' He reached out and took her by the elbow.

She shrugged him away. 'I'm not going anywhere until you tell me what exactly is going on.' An edge of anger tinted her words.

'Whoa! Steady up there, ma'am,' Willard said in a nice-as-pie voice. 'I'm Perry Willard, an agent from the Southern Pacific Rail Road. Sheriff Breen here, he's…'

'The railroad, you say?'

'Yes, ma'am.'

'You have to see my husband 'bout any of that business.' The friendliness had dropped from her tone, a sharp edge replacing it.

'I'm sorry about this, Mary,' Breen said

quietly, looking past her rather than meet her hurt gaze. 'I got me a court writ of eviction. And as from this day, the twentieth of August, eighteen eighty two, this here spread belongs to Mister Heber Carson.' He jerked a thumb over his shoulder. 'The man on the horse.'

Mary's shoulders sagged, she knew it was pointless fighting these men, the railroad had finally defeated them. The sheriff and these men had picked their time well, her husband was away in another part of the valley at a meeting of the Settlers' League and wouldn't return home for hours. She hadn't thought that it would actually come to this but what could she do? She was a woman alone. *No, not alone,* she thought. The girls were playing out in the back yard, she had to be strong for them.

'Ma'am, we'd be obliged if you would start bringing your possessions out of the house,' Willard said. 'I'll help...'

'You won't set one foot inside of this house, mister,' she spat the words at him.

'Just give me the decency to gather the children and what I can before you contaminate our home!'

The words cut into Willard like a whiplash. He had no platitudes for her and he watched helplessly as the rising anger rouged her face.

'Mary, listen to me,' Breen offered, stepping toward her.

'Don't you ever talk to me or mine again, Sheriff Pete Breen!' Her finger shook under his nose. 'As far as we're concerned you ain't no longer a friend. Don't even speak to me or the girls any more.'

Then she was pulling the door to, and pushing past them. They saw tears rolling down her face, and the anger stiffening her joints as she hurried to the backyard.

FIVE

'I'm sorry, but you have been misled.'

The woman sat in a cushioned chair next to an unlit fireplace, a china cup and saucer balanced on her knee, and a bemused look on her face. Time had dealt gently with her; leaving her hair a mousey brown that was plaited into two long pony tails tied with red ribbons; her hazel eyes were as bright as any jack rabbit's as she looked at the two men opposite her. Her rounded face told of good living and she had used minimal make-up expertly applied. Brandon and Slate could not but believe her.

Their morning had been spent asking questions, travelling from one house to another. Their answers had always been the same: 'I hardly knew the man,' or 'That old cuss! Good riddance, I'd say!' or 'A Wife? Who'd be foolish enough to marry that drunkard?' The overall picture that was building up of Butler was not a good one, and as the morning wore on into the afternoon Slate was all for giving up. They halted in an eatery where they dined on antelope steaks with trimmings. Here, an overheard chance remark led them to talking with a teamster. The man, by the name of Three-Fingered Jones, had worked with Butler that spring and he recalled that he had spoken a goodly amount of a woman with her own place about a mile out of town to the northwest on the Santa Cruz River.

Three-Fingered Jones went on to say that Butler was besotted with the woman but she had always laughed off his advances; wanting to marry a rich man and not some buckskin-clad no-hoper. The last Jones had heard of Butler was that he and a kid had headed out to the Santa Rita copper mines to set up a business from the new workings there.

Slate told Three-Fingered Jones of Butler's fate and got better directions to the woman's home, then he and Brandon rode out along the river road until they came to the house. Now, as they drank freshly-ground coffee out of small blue and white china cups, both men felt that the woman was holding out on them. Her large hazel eyes were constantly shifting, unable to settle in one place. She raised her cup to her lips, took a dainty sip, then said, 'Whoever told you that story was lying.'

'Why would he do that?' Slate asked.

'Who knows why people do most things?' she reflected. 'Do you think I am the type of woman who would court a hauler?' She said *hauler* as if it hurt her mouth to say the word.

Brandon admitted to himself that she did have a valid point. Her surroundings suggested that she was used to the finer material things in life. The adobe walls had been plastered and tastefully wallpapered; several framed paintings were hung to take full advantage of the natural light entering the large east facing window; a cut glass chandelier hung from the central mesquite beam. A colourful Navaho rug had been placed in the centre of the room and the furniture arranged around it. Why, indeed, would she bother with a hauler?

Slate said, 'Well, ma'am, you must understand that I had an obligation to honour a dying man's wish.'

'Oh, I do understand, Reverend Slate,' she replied softly. 'It is unfortunate though that you are speaking to the wrong woman.'

'Hmm, guess so, ma'am,' answered Slate.

Brandon finished his drink and placed the cup and saucer down on a highly polished side table. He brought out a cigar saying, 'D'you mind, ma'am?'

She waved a hand for him to continue and he searched his pockets for a lucifer, and not finding one asked, 'Can I trouble you for a light?'

'Over there.' She indicated a box on the mantelpiece.

He pushed himself up from his over-stuffed chair and crossed to the fireplace. As he lit up he looked at a pair of framed tintypes. In one there was a man in his mid-thirties dressed in a Confederate officer's uniform; the other was a woman seated at a table dressed in a long flowing formal dress. The likeness to Alison Rudging, the woman in the room, was uncanny.

'Yes, Mister Brandon,' she said as though reading his mind, 'they are my parents.'

'You favour her very much, ma'am.'

'Why, thank you. She was a beautiful woman. Much loved by myself and Father.' Alison Rudging looked at her mother's portrait and smiled, thinking of happy thoughts from her past.

'Well, gentlemen,' she said brightly, focusing on today. 'I shan't detain you much longer.' She stood up and moved towards the door. 'I'm certain that you'll want to find the *right* woman and give her the lamentable news,' she said with a deep solemnity.

For an instant a faint look of surprise swept across Slate's face, then it was gone. He didn't know how to react to this woman. She gave him a brief smile that set a sparkle in her eyes that age could not dim.

She walked the men to the door and, as she stood there holding it open for them, Slate saw the first faint streaks of grey only beginning to show. There was no denying that she had once been a beauty and the influence of an easy life was evident in her mannerisms, in fact, her whole demeanour.

Alison Rudging waited patiently in the doorway and watched Brandon and Slate walk down the garden path to where they had hitched their horses to her fence. They mounted up, tipped their hats to her and walked the horses off. She watched them until they were dancing figures in the heat haze before she let out her pent-up breath. Once inside the house, she crossed the room to a sideboard and poured herself a healthy amount of French brandy. The liquor was gone in two gulps. She gently placed the balloon glass on the table and said out loud: 'Bastard!'

Mary Jacques led out her team from the barn and harnessed them. Breen, Carson and Willard waited patiently, silently as she completed the chore, then sat in the driver's seat. She held the lines expertly whilst her children climbed onto the seat alongside her. The men could see that she had been crying, her eyes were red-rimmed but still she had no words for them.

The sheriff wasn't comfortable in the task but he realised that whilst the county was paying his wages, he'd have to obey their commands. What he didn't know was how strongly the Settlers' League was affecting the railroad's decision to evict the more prominent figures within the League. As Jacques was their spokesman it naturally fell to him to be the first ousted out of his home.

Mary geed the horses into a walk, driving past the men towards town. The eldest daughter, Paula Anne, lifted her hand to wave at Breen, thought better of it and lowered it into her lap. For her part Mary did not look at the men, she held her head up high but they could see the resignation written across her face. She flicked the lines across the sorrels' backs and stared straight ahead. The men watched as the hastily-laden wagon kicked up a cloud of dust as it followed the rutted road.

They waited until the wagon rounded a bend before Heb Carson brought out a metal hasp and padlock. He fixed this onto the door and gave the key to his partner. Carson felt the weight of it in his hand by throwing it up and catching it. He put it into his jacket pocket and walked his mount around the buildings. Once he had satisfied himself that they were fully secured he said to Willard, 'That's mine fixed up. Now on to yours.'

Willard didn't answer him, content in getting himself comfortable in the sheriff's buggy and waited for the little man to pick up the lines and get the horses into motion. The next homestead was in a neighbouring canyon about a two hour ride away. Willard pulled out a cigar and chewed off the end, lighted it and tipped his hat lower over his eyes. The landscape of short grassland dotted with piñon and white oak was familiar to him so he let them go by unfocused, as were his thoughts.

The sun was still hot and bright as they headed down the road leading into the canyon. They passed a handful of cattle grazing on the taller *sacaton* grass growing near the canyon walls. In the distance they saw more well-fed cattle milling around a grove of cottonwoods near a water hole.

The sight that brought Willard out of his lethargy was the amount of horses and buggies hitched outside the corral. He counted ten saddled mounts and five buggies. He stiffened in the seat and looked over to the sheriff.

'What's happening?' he said sharply.

'I don't rightly know,' Breen answered. 'It looks like they're expecting us.'

'How could they?'

'That's what I'd like to know.'

Heber Carson overheard the exchange and rode closer to the buggy saying, 'I see you've got a welcoming committee, Perry. All of your neighbours coming by to say hello, mayhaps?' He laughed at his own joke.

Neither Breen nor Willard joined him.

Carson dropped his smile, his eyes hardening as he flicked back his jacket behind the handgun and loosened off the thong, then eased the sidearm in its holster. Next he withdrew the carbine from its sheath and jacked a round into the chamber; lowered the hammer and replaced the saddle gun. Only then was he ready for trouble.

Perry Willard picked up his shotgun and leaned it against his leg, barrels pointing downwards. He rested his hand on his thigh, near to the American Arms. It was a precaution best taken because of Carson's unpredictability. He had known Heb to kill a man for looking him the wrong way when he was drunk. He would have killed the man even had he been sober, if he had it in mind.

Sheriff Pete Breen's hands were sweaty, and he was finding it hard to keep a good grip on the lines. The inside of his mouth was as dry as beef jerky and he licked nervously at his lips.

He said, 'I think we might do better to turn back.'

Willard said, 'We've come this far, I can't see the point of turning back now.'

'There's more'n twenty men down there.'

Willard grunted. 'Yeh, but we've got you with us.'

'You think that'll make any difference to them?'

'Shouldn't it? I mean, you're the law around here, aren't you?'

Breen gave a dry cough. 'I know that. But there are some down there who like to think that they're above the law.'

Willard said, 'You trying to tell me that those League men run the show?'

'Hell, no!' Indignation rose in Breen's voice. 'They just like to *think* they do.'

'Just ride in,' Carson joined in, 'and serve him the writ. We'll do the rest.'

'I don't know,' Breen said shaking his head slowly.

'You don't do it,' warned Carson leaning across the saddle, 'I'll blow your fucking head off!'

Breen turned to face Carson and the hard look in the man's eyes said he meant it. He knew that he had no other choice. He flicked the lines across the horses' backs, and rode the buggy downhill toward the main house.

Obviously they had a look-out. As the buggy and the single rider neared the ranch, no more than a hundred or so yards away, the men of the Settlers' League came out of the house and stood around in small groups in the yard. And, of course, Henri Jacques was standing out in front. He wore his best suit with a wide-brimmed Stetson shading his upper face. His thumbs were tucked into his vest pockets as he watched the men approach with great patience.

Breen brought his buggy to a gentle halt in the yard and remained seated. He and Jacques exchanged looks. The settlers' spokesman was puzzled by the sheriff's appearance. He looked at the two strangers with him, not liking what he saw. Jacques broke the silence.

'Sheriff,' he said, nodding to the man. 'Step down and have a cool drink, won't you?'

'Thanks, Henri. That would sure be appreciated.'

'And these men.' He looked at them. 'You're welcome, too.'

Willard, who always seemed to be the spokesman of their partnership, said, 'Obliged to you, but no thanks.'

Jacques gave a non-committal shrug and offered the sheriff the gourd taken from the olla hanging under the ramada. The sheriff drank greedily, spilling drops of cool water down his chin. He dipped the gourd in once again and drank more water. Henri Jacques waited patiently.

When Breen had his fill he wiped a large cotton handkerchief over his mouth, removed his hat and mopped his brow. He reset his hat on his head and looked over the men of the League. There was a great mixture among them: Easterners, Californians and native Arizonans. Each had the right to be here, raising cattle and sheep like the rest of the big ranchers hereabouts, but they were in the way of the S.P.R.R. That, in essence, was the crux of the problem.

'My business is with Bill Skinner,' Breen finally said. He didn't want to talk to Jacques and tell him that his family were on their way into Tucson, along with the fact he had been evicted. He couldn't face that right now.

Breen looked past the spokesman of the Settlers' League and sought out Bill Skinner amongst the crowd. The man standing towards the back, a deep frown creasing his forehead when he heard his name called.

'What do you want me for, sheriff?' he said.

Breen moved among the men and stood opposite the homesteader, having to look up at Skinner as the man was a shade taller than six feet.

'I'd rather speak to you inside, Bill,' Breen said. 'What I've got to say is between you and me.'

'I don't have secrets. These men are my

friends and anything you have to say you can say in front of them.'

Breen sighed. 'Have it your way, then, Bill.' He reached inside his jacket and brought out a folded sheet of paper and offered it to Skinner. 'I'm issuing you with a writ of eviction served on this day of August by the power of the Southern Pacific Rail Road on whose land you reside.'

Skinner looked at him for a minute. He didn't know whether to laugh or cry. His long, thin face showed bemusement which slowly turned to anger.

'Hell, Breen, you gone loco?' he shouted. 'This your idee of a joke?'

'No, Bill,' the sheriff replied, shifting uneasily from one foot to another. 'It's all official and written up in this sheet of paper.'

Skinner snatched the legal document from the man's hand and began to rip it into little shreds, then threw them into Breen's face.

Perry Willard watched the crowd for their reaction. Every other man was toting a weapon of some kind: mainly handguns with the odd rifle or two; one man was leaning on a two prong pitchfork but no one had ventured a hand towards using any of the weapons. Carefully placing his shotgun to one side, he stepped down out of the buggy and stood loose-limbed watching over the sheriff.

Breen swallowed hard. 'It doesn't matter if you rip that one up, Bill, there's another lodged in the courthouse back in town. If you took the time to read it, it said that you've got to clear out right now.'

'Like hell…'

'You've enough time to move out all your possessions and such, but the property now belongs to Mister Willard.'

Skinner looked over to the man standing by the buggy. His eyes searching for some kind of emotion on the man's face.

'You bought my place from under me, mister?' he asked.

'Yeah, I bought it,' Willard replied. 'The railroad offered it up at a reasonable price.'

'You ain't got the right, it's mine by law!'

Breen said, 'No. No, it's not. I thought that

you might understand what has been going on the last few months. Even Henri here must've warned you all.' He turned to the man. 'You *have* been telling them what the railroad offered haven't you?'

'It's all been above board,' Jacques said. 'These men know the way the Big Four fight, and we need more time at the courts to fight back.'

Jacques was talking about the big financiers of the Southern Pacific Rail Road: Charles Crocker, Collis Huntington, Leland Stanford and Mark Hopkins.

'I'm sorry about this. I really am, but you've go no choice in the matter.' Breen sounded genuinely sorry and made to move off. Skinner caught his shoulder in a heavy grip and spun him around to face him.

'You've got to give me more time!' he pleaded. 'I've over two hundred head of cattle out there and more wild uns up in the high medders. You've *got* to give me the chance to gather them in.'

'They belong to me as well,' Willard said.

Skinner shook his head in amazement. 'I don't believe it! What right have you got to buy a man's land then take away his cattle? Uh? Answer me that!'

Willard looked the man hard in the eye. His cold stare clashed against the heat of anger.

'Sheriff,' Jacques interrupted. 'I believe you owe it to us to appeal against this conviction. We can go to the Supreme Court on this. You know it's not ethical.'

'Ethical be damned!' Carson spoke up for the first time. 'The way I see it, you're in the same corral as him,' he said stabbing a finger at Skinner.

'What do you mean?'

A smile split Carson's thin lips like that of a snake's mouth. 'I've just bought your place.'

The words hit Jacques with the force of a blow between the yes. He felt a sudden tightening in his chest. Bile rose to his throat and he swallowed the bitterness down before he let out a yell of rage, and lunged at the horseman. Sheriff Breen acted quickly for a man his size and barred Jacques' way with his body. He grabbed him by his suit lapels and wrestled him still.

'Henri! Henri, listen up, man!' He shouted in his face and shook him till the Settlers' League man turned to face him. 'I'll give you that time. For pity's sake don't do anything hasty. We'll leave peaceably and go back to town.'

Jacques composed himself smartly and nodded his agreement, his face pale and blank, eyes staring off unfocused into the distance. When Breen felt Jacques' body relax he let his lapels go and smoothed out the jacket for him.

'Sheriff,' Willard said, 'I don't recall you having the power to negate any of these convictions.'

Breen stepped over to face the gunfighter, suddenly feeling brave enough to face the gunsel. He squared up to Willard and said, 'I've been telling you all along that I'm the law and what I say goes. These men are entitled to an appeal and I'll see that they get it, savvy?'

Willard closed his eyes and nodded slowly. There was a fierce conviction in the sheriff's voice and he knew that he had lost the argument.

'You'd better get this, Jacques!' Carson called out as he drew out his Colt and fired a shot.

The slug thwacked into the man's upper chest and knocked him onto the floor. A second slug tore through the side of his head extinguishing his life instantly.

Gunsmoke hung in the air and the suddenness of the murder immobilised the crowd. Breen was the first to react, and he moved to confiscate Willard's shotgun. The gunfighter was quicker and he brought the butt down onto the sheriff's nose.

Breen was cowkilled. His nose cartilage burst apart, spraying blood like water from a fountain. The sheriff fell to the floor, hands covering his face, moaning and rolling about.

Willard swung the shotgun barrels at the crowd and fired at a man going for his side-arm. The settler had barely put his hand on the grips when the shotgun barrel barked loudly and spewed fire, smoke and pellets. From that distance the effect was devastating. The man's head disintegrated from his shoulders, showering blood and gore over those close by.

Willard's face was splattered with blood and brain matter. He could taste the warm blood on his lips as he shifted the shotgun and pulled the trigger again. The man who held the pitchfork was cut in two before he could raise the weapon any further.

He had reacted to the violence without a further thought, and mentally cursed Carson for reacting so impulsively. There could be no turning back now. The settlers would give them no pity and Willard knew that it might be a fight to the death.

Carson began to fire repeatedly into the crowd, not caring if any of the men were armed or not. In a matter of thirty seconds men were lying dead and wounded. Those who were quick enough to gather their wits about them began to run for cover. One man who had been wounded in the chest was running away when Carson fired again and backshot him. An evil, dead-eyed smile crossed his face as he watched the man twitching on the floor in his death throes.

Willard thumbed new shells into the shotgun and let loose both barrels towards a group of cowering men, then threw it down and drew out his .45. The returning fire wasn't accurate but enough to make him seriously seek out cover. He snatched a glance to his right and saw a big barn with its doors open. Fanning the hammer he gave himself enough covering fire to dash the fifty feet to the safety of the barn.

Heber Carson was enjoying himself, prancing up and down on his horse firing indiscriminately at the men. Once he had emptied his revolver he drew out the Winchester carbine and began using that. He was satisfied when he heard his shots find their targets and the high-pitched squeals that filled the air. He was taking aim at a man hiding behind a water trough when his horse was shot from under him.

He reacted quickly. Kicking his feet free of the stirrups he landed upright, and still managed to fire the Winchester. But he was now left in the open and began to draw some serious attention. A slug creased his right thigh, stinging him. A second tugged at his sleeve.

Now, he thought, *it was time to be leaving.*

Carson fired a couple of shots to keep the men's heads down as he made a beeline for the horses hitched to the corral fence. He picked out a good looking dun and boosted himself into the saddle. He quickly looked around for his partner and heard the shooting coming from the barn. He took the reins to the neighbouring sorrel and dallied them around the saddle horn. Viciously he rowelled the dun and headed for the barn.

He had covered half the distance before a red-headed Leaguer stepped out from behind the main house and fired his Sharps .50 buffalo rifle at point-blank range. The big-calibre bullet hit Carson under his rib cage and punched a large exit hole in his back. The shot lifted him out of the saddle and he bounced across the back of the sorrel and landed dead, on the ground.

Perry Willard watched as his partner somersaulted out of the saddle and lay unmoving in the dirt. A dark stain was already spreading over the ground beneath him. Willard took aim at the red-head who was busy jumping around in jubilation, and calmly shot him through the heart.

'That's for Heb, you friggin' sonofabitch!' he spat. The remaining Settlers' League men with only one target left to fire at, began to concentrate their lead at Willard.

Slugs smacked against the heavy oak doors, but not penetrating them. Willard checked his belt for spare cartridges and found to his horror that he had only eight left. He fired off a couple of shots that hit nobody, then reloaded. He had to think of a way to survive this fight.

He looked around the barn for the first time. There was no back way out, and the only other way was through the hay loft. He knew it was foolish place to hide as they'd only have to torch the place to get him.

He moved deeper into the gloomy interior and concentrated on a plan of escape. As soon as he saw it the plan was quickly formulated: leaning against the wall was a sledge hammer. He holstered his gun and hefted the long-handled hammer shoulder-high, and moving to the rear of the barn he took an almighty swing at the wooden planking. An upright splintered under the force of the blow and he took a second swing. The plank next to it shattered and sunlight burst through the hole which was big enough for him to get through.

He was out on the other side and running before anyone ventured near the barn. He angled across the ground, keeping the barn behind him and ran as hard as he could heading for the tree line.

SIX

Jim Brandon and Reverend Slate arrived back in Tucson too late for Butler's funeral. The men went over to speak to Father Weller to find out who had turned up to pay their last respects; Three-Fingered Jones and two miners were the only mourners. Slate mentally cursed himself for missing it and sat in a rocker on the hotel's verandah. He took out a recently purchased Long Nine, a favourite cigar, and lit up.

Brandon took the chair next to him and watched the town's people parade past. He knew by the look on Slate's face that he was in no mood for conversation, and by his own admission, he didn't have much to say anyway. Everything had come to a dead end. He brought out a deck of cards from his jacket pocket and began to shuffle them casually. His thoughts went back to Alison Rudging.

She had said that she didn't know Butler, let alone been his sweetheart. Perhaps this was a flight of fancy on Butler's part; his feelings for her might have only been distant admiration. He could have seen her about town and gotten the notion that one day she might accept him as her gentleman caller.

But what did he have to offer her? Nothing much as far as Brandon could tell. A germ of an idea was beginning to grow in Brandon's head. He had to speak with Slate no matter what his mood, and voice his notions.

'Joe, I've been thinking,' he began and stopped shuffling the cards to turn and face the reverend. 'Let's suppose that Butler knew Alison. Maybe not intimately but seen her from afar and got it into his head that he was in love with her.'

'Bit fanciful wouldn't you say?'

'Yeah, but say if he *did*. What would he possibly have to interest her?'

Slate said, 'I doubt if he had anything.'

'Land?'

'Nope.'

'A home?'

'Nothing that would equal hers.'

Brandon went on. 'How about money?'

Slate shook his head. 'I doubt it.'

'Where is she getting hers?'

Slate pulled a face and finger-combed his beard. 'For all we know, she may not need any cash.'

'So where does her money come from?' persisted Brandon.

Like it or not, the reverend was being forced out of his sulk, and the gambler's questions were beginning to intrigue him. 'You saying that she and Butler did have something going between them?'

'Yeah, I do,' Brandon replied. 'Let's say that they knew each other and Butler was out to impress her one way or another. Her kind of woman needs a lot of looking after, and we've seen the life style she likes; fanciful china and crystal chandeliers, and the such. That kind of upkeep takes a lot of money and I suspicion that she's up to something.'

'Such as?'

'Ah, that's where my thoughts end,' he said.

'You wouldn't consider the notion that she may be a widow?'

That thought hadn't crossed Brandon's mind, and if she was a rich widow...

'Maybe *he* was after *her* money,' he ventured.

'Hell, Jim. You don't give up do you?'

'Well now, Joe, seems like you're the one who got us started off in the first place. It's got me interested, and I'd like to delve a little further.'

Slate puffed on the cigar and blew out a cloud of smoke. 'I'll tell you what. How about if we go along to Father Weller and ask him? He seems the kind of man who takes an interest in his flock, wouldn't you say?'

'He's already told us he knows nothing about Alison and Butler being together.'

Slate looked at Brandon a little blankly.

He knew that this was an area they had already looked into, but he was sure he was missing something along the way.

Brandon jumped to his feet, snapping his fingers. 'Hey, I just remembered something! That sheriff back in Flower Creek knew Butler, didn't he?' His voice was tight with excitement. 'What if you go see Father Weller and I send a telegram to Flower Creek, uh? Say I meet you back in the saloon in an hour or so?'

Slate smiled and said, 'I don't think we're all that popular with that sheriff, do you?'

'We helped him out with Butler, didn't we?'

'Suppose he might help but I wouldn't bet on it.'

It was Brandon's turn to smile. 'Leave the betting to me, eh?'

Slate shook his head slowly, cringing at the pun.

'Let's say we meet up in the saloon at three. That should give us enough time to get things sorted out.'

Slate gave him a little disapproving look, knowing what saloon Brandon was talking about, and said, 'OK, but don't go disappearing with that little gal if I'm late.'

'As if I would.'

'Given half the chance…'

Joe Slate turned his mount into the alleyway that led to the rear of Our Lady's church. A frown crumpled his forehead when a trio of men walked across the mouth of the alley, blocking his exit. He rode forward and met them head on. The bigger man in the middle silently held up his hand to halt Slate. The reverend stopped and slowly turned around to check his back, there was no one there, then turned back, putting both hands on the saddle-horn and waited. Away in the distance a dog began barking, followed by a deep voice shouting at it to shut up followed by a crash, then a yelp. Silence filled the garbage-ridden alleyway, thick like a helping of molasses.

Slate remained silent, waiting for one of

the men to have his say. He looked at each one of them in turn. They were dressed in rough workman-like clothing, each wore a hat that shaded their faces and all carried handguns, but there was nothing to suggest they were professionals, and besides, Slate thought, who would be out to kill him?

The big man stepped away from his companions, one hand on his gun, but leaving it holstered. He stopped a few feet away from Slate, stood cock-hipped and said,

'Get down, reverend.'

Slate was calm when he said, 'Why?'

'Jest do as I tell you, uh?' came the harsh reply.

Slate looked at the man, noticing the nervous twitch in his eyes, and the constant licking of his lips. 'What do you want?' he said, still not moving.

'Why don't we just shoot him and have done, Billy?'

The man in front, Billy, turned his head and said, 'Keep that big mouth of yourn shut, Joel. I'm dealing with it, all right?'

'Hey, Billy! What's this all about?' Slate asked.

Billy turned around surprised at the reverend sounding so friendly. 'Why don't you do as you're tolt an' get off the horse?'

Slate remained seated, watching Billy and especially Joel, seeing that the man wanted him dead. He said to Billy, 'C'mon, Billy. What're you doing holding up a man of the cloth? I ain't got nothing on me worth taking. Everything I've got is on my back and this horse. I got no cash.'

'Listen, preacher man,' Joel said. 'We want *you*. Savvy?'

Slate figured that the whole thing was getting out of hand. These men didn't want his money or horse, for some reason they wanted him, and that aroused both his curiosity and his anger. He kept a calm appearance as he feigned surprise.

'Me? What do you want with me?'

Billy said, 'I don't want to shoot you, but iffen you don't get off that horse, then, by God I will.'

He still hadn't taken his gun out. Slate was busy working out the options. If he did get off his horse, they'd crowd him but if he didn't, he'd be shot off. Where was the choice? He sat for a minute in silence, looking the men over; deciding that Joel was the dangerous one, the man at the back with the almost white hair was their lookout and Billy was the spokesman. He dropped out of the saddle but still held onto the reins. Slate's clear blue eyes narrowed. 'You planning on killing me?'

'Depends.'

'Yeah, on what?'

'On what you know.'

Billy pushed Joel aside and snapped at him, 'What did I say 'bout that big mouth of yourn?'

Joel glared at him and moved off to lean against the side of a wall. His long, thin face was dark with anger and Slate could see he was just itching to use the .44 tucked into his waistband but obviously wasn't prepared to override Billy's orders. The third man remained silent and kept his position at the top of the alleyway. Slate coldly looked Billy over: round-faced, chin whiskers, large nose and deep brown eyes, and committed those features to memory.

'Seems you've been poking your nose into business that doesn't concern you,' Billy began. 'Heard tell that you've been trying to stir up a hornets' nest of trouble.'

'Have I now?' Slate wanted Billy to talk more, finding out where he was coming from and if he meant him any real danger.

Billy jabbed a finger at Slate's chest. 'Yeh, you and your pardner have trod on some toes. And the people them toes belong to don't like it none, you savvy?'

Slate remained silent.

Billy went on. 'Now these here persons want you to leave town, an' quit botherin' 'em, understand?'

'Go on, what else?'

'If you decide not to co-operate like, then we'd have to deal with you.'

'You threatening me … er … us, is that it?'

'In a nutshell, mister,' Joel said.

'As a man of the cloth, I'm expected to turn the other cheek to violence and other such uncouthness, but I don't take lightly to having my life, or my partner's threatened by a couple of down at heels. I could get annoyed and then do something silly.'

Billy was confused and said, 'What're you jabberin' about?'

'You and your *compadres* are the noisome pestilence and the terror of the night, and you will be swept off the face of the earth.'

Joel pushed himself away from the wall, his hand on the grips of his .44, saying, 'That's mightly big talk coming from a man who don't carry no gun. I say waste him now Billy, and have done with ii.'

Billy sighed. 'No, not yet we can't. We got to find out what he knows.'

'About what?' Slate asked.

Billy finally drew out his revolver and pointed it at Slate, thumbing back the hammer. 'What did Butler tell you?'

'Ah, now we get down to it, eh?' His and Brandon's involvement with the hauler was at the bottom of this encounter. Had Butler told him something which was of any importance to these men, or did someone else who hired them think he had?

'I'm going to read you something out of the good book, OK?' He slowly reached into his pocket and brought out a battered leather-bound copy of the Bible. He thumbed through the pages to find the passage he was after and then began to read aloud.

'Don't turn this into a ser...' The final word, 'sermon', was snatched from his lips as Slate battered the Bible across Billy's face. Once, twice, then a third time. The blows forced him sideways on to Slate.

In a fast manoeuvre, Slate snatched the Colt from Billy's hand and swung his free arm around Billy's neck, pulling him backwards in a head lock. The Colt was aimed at the startled Joel before he had the time to react to the situation.

'I've got a gun now, Joel. What you planning on doing about it? Still want to kill me, eh?'

'Don't, Joel!' rasped Billy.

'C'mon, you can do it,' egged Slate.

'Billy?' Joel whined.

'Don't even think about it, Joel,' Billy spluttered.

Slate caught a movement from the end of the alleyway and looked around. The white-haired would-be thug had made off in all the confusion. Good, that was one less for him to think about.

'So, Joel, what're we going to do?' Slate was pushing him. 'If you shoot me, you'll have to shoot Billy as well. Are you that good a shot to try it?'

Joel still had his hand on the gun but something was stopping him using it.

Slate grinned slyly. 'You know I can shoot you and call it self-defence. What have you got to say about that?'

'You'd never get away with it,' Billy said.

'Oh, that's easy, son. I'll say something like: "It was like this sheriff, three men tried to roll me in the alley; one ran away, I shot one going for his gun and the other was killed in the ruckus". Simple, eh?'

'You wouldn't, would you?' asked Billy.

'Try me and see.'

A tense silence filled with electricity enveloped the men. Slate kept the head lock on Billy and Joel still had his hand on his gun. Neither party wanted to make the first, and perhaps fatal, move. Slate could see the troubled look in Joel's dark eyes. He had undoubtedly thought that things were going to be so easy he hadn't expected any opposition from the white-bearded, dirty man with straw-coloured hair facing him down.

The reverend spoke up. 'There's an easy way out of this, fellers. You tell me who sent you and I'll let you go free.'

Joel seemed to have made up his mind. 'You wouldn't use that gun, reverend.'

'You calling my bluff, youngster?'

He took a deep breath and said, 'Yeah, that's what I'm doing.'

Joel began to remove the .44 from his waistband. Slate watched him until he had nearly completed the draw, then fired. The bullet hit the earth between his feet, whanged off the wall and ricocheted down the alley. Joel jumped back, colliding with the wall and dropped his gun as if he had touched the business end of a running iron.

'Gooddarn! You would, too!' he exclaimed, fear flecking his eyes.

Slate eared back the hammer and pressed the muzzle into the loose flesh under Billy's chin.

'You've tried my patience, and I'm near the very end of it.' His voice was a hoarse whisper. 'Tell me who hired you to jump me. Now!'

Billy shook his head, well as much as he could with the head lock on.

'Don't be heroic, Billy. A ten spot ain't much to die for so I'll ask you just one more time – who?'

Joel said, 'Iffen you don't tell him, Billy, I sure as hell will.'

'OK! OK! Three-Fingered Jones put us up to it.' His words were running into each other, he was wanting to get them out that quick. 'He told us that Butler had made some cash working at the Santa Rita mines, and he told you and that gambler where he stashed it. Said if we found out where he hid it, then he would split it with us.'

'Come on, Billy, you think I'm going to swallow that?' Slate replied wearily and pushed the barrel deeper into his chin. 'Why didn't Jones do his own dirty work?'

'I don't know. Honest. You've got to believe me.'

Slate didn't, but obviously he wasn't going to get the whole truth out of either Billy or Joel. He pushed Billy away from him, the Colt covering both men.

'Empty the shells from your gun, Joel,' he ordered and waited until it was carried out, then said, 'If I ever see your faces in town again, I'll reconsider about killing you. Understand?'

'Yeah, sure reverend,' Billy stammered.

'Whatever you want.' The bravado had gone from Joel's voice, he knew that he was getting off with his life and was anxious to get out of the alley.

'Now *vamos*, and remember what I said. And yeah, don't pay Jones a visit, let him stew awhiles, I'll deal with him later. Now git out of here.' He waved the Colt at the two men.

They ran down the alley as fast as their legs could carry them, sped around the corner out of sight, and gun range. Slate held on to the Colt and waited a minute or two before returning to his horse. He still had business with Father Weller and this little incident was like pouring oil on troubled water.

A month ago he was happily travelling around the country, minding his own business until he came across a wounded Jim Brandon and a troubled Mexican beauty named Karla Luz. She had been nursing him back to health from a bullet graze he'd received as he tried to protect her travelling companion who had been kidnapped by a ruthless gang of cutthroats. Both he and Brandon went after the men, not for any reward but because they were, in their own way, honour-bound: Brandon because he had formed an attachment to Karla, and Slate because of his own self-confessed calling.

They had come out of the scrap intact and by the end of it an easy friendship had started up. By mutual consent they chose to travel together, heading to the Yellowstone National Park which was Slate's original intention before joining forces with the gambler. What happened after they got there, he didn't know, but he did know that this was the second bout of trouble he'd been involved in since siding with Brandon.

His cavalry training had kept him alive in hostile country for years, but he hadn't had to use a gun so much in such a short time. The anger was burning low in his gut and he knew it would only be a short time until it would boil over and erupt into violence. He looked down at the confiscated Colt, a good-looking ivory-handled Peacemaker, and sighed heavily. Back in the hotel his own single holster gunbelt and an oiled Colt .45 were protected with muslin. He didn't care much for wearing a rig, but whoever had hired these men through Jones seemed to mean business, so the decision to buckle it on had been made for him.

He was not sure how Three-Fingered Jones actually fitted into the situation and he mulled the question over in his mind for a while. By his own admission Jones knew Butler, and even attended the funeral this morning. Now he seemed to be behind this farcical hold-up attempting to get information out of Slate with a cock-and-bull story of hidden loot. No, all in all it didn't quite gel; a man like Jones would have done his own dirty work. Slate considered that there must be someone else who put Jones up to it.

The question was who?

The answer to that one, Slate thought, had to wait.

Brandon looked at his watch: 2.45 pm and still no sign of Slate.

'You goin' some'ers, Jim?' The man asking him the question sat opposite, one hand covering his cards, the other holding a drink but his eyes were steady and clear.

'Waiting for someone to come,' Brandon replied easily.

They were playing a hand of poker, dealer's choice with no wild cards, and Brandon was dealing. He skimmed the cards across the table and waited for the calls. There was something wrong with his game today, he couldn't maintain his concentration. The wire he sent to Flower Creek hadn't been answered yet and that gnawed away in the back of his mind.

He had lost a couple of hands through stupid mistakes but because they were playing for dollar ante stakes it didn't bother him none. He made up his mind that if Joe had not appeared by their agreed time, he'd throw in his cards and go back over to the telegraph office to find out what was happening.

The game was won by a bearded storekeeper and Brandon gave up the deal to leave the table. Someone else was eager to take his place even before the chair had a chance to get cold. He bellied up to the bar, ordered a beer and helped himself to a pickled egg from the jar which he devoured in a couple of bites, then he ordered a beef sandwich.

The food came at the same time as the skinny, tow-haired errand boy from the telegraph office. He pushed his way through the swing doors, eyes searching across the mass of bodies for Brandon. The gambler called him over, tipped him a couple of cents, and eagerly tore open the reply from Sheriff Bell. He read it through a couple of times before he remembered the boy was waiting for a reply.

'No reply yet, son,' he said. 'I'll be over shortly with my answer, thanks.'

The young lad shrugged his shoulders and went back to work. Brandon folded the telegram, finished his food and beer, then digging out his timepiece he saw that Slate was twenty minutes late and decided to go over to the church.

Brandon met Slate half-way across the

street. They turned their horses toward their hotel and exchanged their news.

Brandon went first. 'The reply came back from Bell.'

'And?'

'And Bell figures that if Butler was married to someone in Tucson he didn't know about it. But you remember the youngster that was killed with him? Turns out that it was his son.'

'His *what?*'

'Yeah, that's what I thought.'

Slate shook his head. 'The man's got a son and no one knows who his wife is? That sounds mighty peculiar to me. How did Bell know the kid was his son?'

Brandon shrugged his shoulders. 'Damned if I know. There seems to be too many questions and not enough answers to go around.'

'I agree with you there, Jim.'

They halted outside the corral behind the hotel and off-saddled. The men were quiet; thinking about the news from the sheriff and how best to deal with the situation.

'How did it go with Father Weller?' asked Brandon as they walked back down the alley to the hotel.

'Oh, him! I swear that he wouldn't know one end of a branding iron to the other!'

'By that I take it you had a wasted trip?'

Slate smiled wryly. 'Not entirely.'

They stopped on the walkway in front of the hotel's main doors. The sun was high in the sky and baked everything beneath it. Slate turned and looked down the busy street. Downtown some of the stores were just opening up from siesta time, others had pulled down their blinds to keep the interiors cool. There wasn't a breath of good, cooling air to be had anywhere and the reverend ran a finger around his sticky collar, loosening it slightly.

'C'mon, Joe, the suspense is killing me. What happened?'

'I was held up.'

It was Brandon's turn to show disbelief. 'Held up! Tell me about it, man.'

Slate put a hand on Brandon's shoulder

and said, 'Calm down, Jim. Nothing really happened. Well, nothing that I couldn't handle. Three yahoos stopped me in an alleyway and demanded that I tell them about Butler's hidden cache of money.'

'His *what?*' Brandon sat down heavily into the rocker, a look of bewilderment plastered across his face. 'What's going on here, Joe? First we got us a mysterious wife, then out of the woodwork pops a son and now ... now hidden loot. What the hell's going to happen next?'

Slate sighed and shrugged his massive shoulders. 'I only wish I knew,' he said wist-fully.

'Why did they try and bushwhack you, though?'

'Ah, seems our friend Three-Fingered Jones, set them up to do the job.'

'Jones? No, I don't believe it.'

'Nor do I, if that's any consolation. I reckon that we ought to pay him a visit.'

'Yeah, I'm behind you on that one. Why the little snakey sonofabitch. I'll make him squeal. He could have got you killed!'

'No worries on that, Jim.'

'Say, what did happen to them fellers who jumped you?' Brandon wanted to know.

Again, that smile from Slate. 'Oh, I showed them the errors of their ways with the help from my Bible.'

'You didn't preach 'em to death, did you?' Brandon laughed, trying to take the gravity out of the situation.

'Something like that,' Slate answered. 'But we'd better be on the lookout for one of them fellers. He was mighty quick to want to fill me full of lead. I reckon he's one of those sneaky little boogers who'll creep up to you in the dark and slit your throat.'

'Yeah, we'd best be on our guard, then.'

SEVEN

Perry Willard's shirt was ripped in several places but he didn't mind. The seat of his pants had split under the crotch and he couldn't care less. He jarred his knee leaping over a deadfall but still didn't worry. He had only six bullets left and that scared the hell out of him.

He had made it to the timberline before the first of the Settlers' League men stepped out of the hole he had made in the barn. For a moment or two there was confusion as to which way he went. As Willard bent double gasping for breath he watched one of the men slowly walking around the outside of the barn, stop every now and again to bend down and examine something. A moment or two later he straightened up and seemed to look at the very spot where Willard stood.

Willard didn't believe there was a tracker amongst the Leaguers but he cursed his luck that there might have been. With the tables turned against him, with Carson dead, and the sheriff agin him, Willard's luck was looking bleak.

He leant back against a tree and flipped open the .45's gate and took out one cartridge. He turned the cylinder so that the hammer dropped onto the empty chamber and reholstered it. He took out his sack of tobacco and dropped the cartridge in and repocketed it.

Sweat was cooling his face as he waited for a moment, thinking. Obviously the Leaguers were going to be mounted, but the trees were quite dense and impenetrable in places. All he had to do was to get himself deeper into the timber and wait for night to come. He pushed himself away from the tree and began weaving his way up the hill, the sounds of his clumsy passing masked the soft but insistent drum of approaching hoofbeats.

His thighs were beginning to burn with

the exertion of hauling himself up the steep gradient and sweat trickled between his shoulder blades, plastering his cheap cotton shirt to his back. The day was growing cooler and Willard guessed the time to be around five or thereabouts.

The thick canopy of green leaves hid most of the sun's rays making this part of the hillside dark and smelling of rotting leaves. He had taken a rest a while ago when he stopped to listen for any sounds of his hunters. He had heard the snorting of a filly mare and a few wind-snatched words but the trees buffeted any ordinary sounds.

He figured that the riders couldn't pick their way through the trees and were wandering around aimlessly. Willard had pushed onwards and upwards, now he was aching to stop, just needing to sit down and roll a smoke and rest awhiles. His throat was swollen, his lips cracked and dried, and the hunger pains that gnawed in his stomach made him feel sick. He dropped to the forest floor, the smoke forgotten, and rolled up into a ball.

How long he had been asleep for he didn't know, and for a spell he was disorientated in his new surroundings. It had been years since he had slept out in the open. He had gotten too used to plump mattresses and warm female company. The dampness had seeped into his bones and made him shiver involuntarily. The light had almost bled from the sky and a fresh wind had picked up, scuttling dead leaves along the ground that sounded like skeletal bones rattling he had once heard.

Willard began searching around for dry wood and kindling to make himself a fire. Ten minutes of scrambling around had brought him a pile of dead wood that should at least get him warm. It took a couple of lucifers to fire the kindling and he bundled a pyramid of wood around it. He didn't make a big fire that might betray his position but one large enough to get himself warm. As he waited he rolled himself a couple of smokes and got as close as he could to the fire. His only worry was where he could get food and water.

He decided that he had no choice but to get down out of the timbers after he had got warm again, and look for a homestead and take whatever he wanted. He knew if he couldn't get any food or water up here he would die anyway, and the thought of starving to death frightened him more than facing someone with a pistol. Satisfied with that solution he became a little relaxed and began to enjoy his smoke.

Brandon and Slate walked out of the Chinese restaurant just as the sun was dipping behind the buildings to the west of town. Their long shadows danced crazily before them on the hard-packed ground as they began heading back to their hotel. They felt well-rested and relaxed as the fresh, early evening wind blew down the street cooling them when they stopped next to the restaurant's hitching rail. Brandon's stomach was full to the brim with noodles and pan-fried chicken. Slate had chosen a beef dish with thick onion gravy and bell peppers with rice.

He pulled out a Long Nine, bit the end off, then lit up. He savoured the heavy aroma for a second, turned to Slate and said, 'There's that game on tonight at the Congress Hall Saloon. I reckon I might join in. You got any objections? I guess that we can pick up on things come the morning. It's not likely we can achieve anything tonight, is it?'

Slate grinned and replied, '"Be not overcome by evil, but overcome evil with goodness".'

Brandon pursed his lips, thought for a moment, then said, 'OK, tell me what that means.'

'Well you can take it a couple of ways, like two faces of a coin, but what I'm trying to tell you is that you should win without cheating.'

Brandon faked indignation. 'Me? Cheat? No, never.'

Slate had a curious look in his eyes, stared back and resisted the temptation to laugh out loud. After all, he had seen Brandon play poker before. Instead, he clapped a hand on the gambler's shoulder and shook his head. They headed off towards Camp Street, just a couple of blocks away. They hadn't gone but a few yards when Slate stretched out a restraining hand across Brandon's chest.

'Forget the game!' he said. 'Come with me. I've just seen someone I recognise, and we need to have a talk. *Buqui,* come on.'

Slate refused to answer Brandon's persistent questions as they began to follow two men dressed in working clothes along the street at a discreet distance. Slate and Brandon took full advantage of the darkening day, using a shop doorway to hide in when one of the men stopped to take a leak behind a tree. Then they were off again, turning left into Camp Street and walked up to Brown's Congress Hall Saloon and shops. Brandon felt a little tug of regret that he was missing out on the game, but one glance at Slate's determined expression provided him with the answer to his unvoiced question.

They continued shadowing the two men

until the former had reached the County Courthouse and stopped. Here they exchanged a few words, then separated. Slate nudged Brandon in the ribs, his head nodding towards the man walking away from the courthouse.

'Good, Jim. *Buqui.*'

He grunted his assent, still miffed about not knowing why they were following the shambling figure ahead as he turned away from the courthouse, making his way towards the Presidio wall. Here the streets became narrower and more crowded as men and women wandered from taverna to taverna. It was obvious that the man, drunk as he seemed, was heading towards his favourite watering-hole. The man they were following stopped half-way down the street outside a taverna, and without a glance in his pursuers' direction walked through the adobe archway entering the place. Slate and Brandon waited for a moment, listening to guitar music and to the men and women standing in the small courtyard talking loudly above the music, then followed.

Inside the noise was incessant as waves pounding on the sea shore. Mexican and Anglo men and women mixed easily, shouting loud just to be heard; beer slopped from glasses and hit the tiled floor with dull splatters. The gambler and the preacher looked about them and found their quarry leaning against the bar with a half-filled jug in front of him, trying as best as he could to stop himself from swaying. Slate looked pointedly at him and Brandon followed his gaze. The man lifted the glass unsteadily to his lips; he only had three fingers on that hand.

Slate leaned towards Brandon. 'You remember Three-Fingered Jones, the jasper who hired them men to bushwhack me? Well, there he is and I couldn't miss this opportunity to question him, could I?' His eyes were beaming with pleasure.

Brandon nodded and replied, 'No, not at all.'

They pushed their way through the crowd, with Slate standing in front of Jones whilst

Brandon took up a space at the bar behind him. The gambler caught the man's personal rank odour made more cloying in the closeness of the taverna. He looked around; others were calling for drinks and food from the two barmen, others barged their way up to the bar uncaring of who they shouldered out of the way. Brandon picked up the succulent aroma of baked ham and looking down the bar saw platters of roast beef, pickles, pig's feet and a slab of white Sonora cheese. His mouth watered at the sight.

'Hello, Jones,' Slate began. 'I told you, I'd catch up with you.'

The man looked up. It took him a few seconds to focus his eyes on the man towering over him. A face that was encased in a beard with blond hair poking out beneath a brown wide-brimmed Plainsman hat. When Jones spoke his words were slurred and hesitant.

'What do you want with me? I ain't done you no harm, have I?'

'A few words is all.'

'Uh! I got nothin' to say to you,' Three-Fingered Jones said, raising his beer to his lips. Slate's right hand snaked out and caught Jones's wrist in a tight grip.

'Oh, we have. We can talk of those higher than us. *Comprende?*'

Jones's brow creased in puzzlement. 'I got no idea of what you're talkin' about.'

'I wouldn't say that,' Slate replied easily and released his grip on Jones. He called out his order to a passing barkeep. Once they came Slate raised his glass.

'To Butler, long may we remember his poor, simple soul,' he toasted.

Three-Fingered Jones grinned, his teeth dull in the sickly yellow lantern light. 'In a pig's eye!' he hissed.

'Now, friend, tell me what you mean by that.'

'Why should I?'

Slate leant closer, whispering in Jones's ear, 'If you do, you'll leave this place a richer man.'

'An' sposing I don't?'

The reverend's hard blue eyes narrowed as he fixed a grim smile on Three-Fingered Jones. 'Then my friend, you'll be making an early acquaintance with your Maker. But let's not talk of violence. We can be friends, can't we? There's money to be earned by all so let us exchange information. What do you know?'

The drunken teamster looked hard into Slate's face, his eyes watering in the smoke-laden atmosphere. The reverend took out a gold alazana, a Mexican gold coin, and pushed it along the counter towards Jones. The drunk's hand slapped down hard over the coin and swept it into his pocket in one easy motion.

'First off, I want to hear who hired you to scare off me an' my partner,' Slate said easily.

Three-Fingered Jones gulped down the remains of his first beer, wiped away the froth from his mouth with the back of his sleeve then said, 'I was haulin' some timber for Father Weller later that day you brung Butler in an' the father told me about how you and that gambler feller brung him in from Flower Creek. He asked if I knew anythin' about him, an' I said I didn't. You see, word had gotten around that he had struck it lucky at the copper mine at Santa Rita. An' there was one time I saw him with a pouch filled with gold an' silver coins an' a bundle of notes this thick.' He made a sizeable circle with his thumb and fore-finger.

'We've been all through this before. Stop foolin' around, there's more. Tell me who paid you to set about me and my partner.'

'Not here!' Three Fingered Jones hissed. He gazed around the crowded tavern. 'Outside, there're too many ears here.'

Joe Slate eased himself away from the bar, waited for Jones to drain off his beer, then both pushed their way out into the court-yard. The evening air was heavy with the scent of honeysuckles which grew in large pots and trailed their way across some trellis work. Other folk were outside enjoying the fresh air; a group of men were playing pinochle whilst couples talked in quiet, secretive tones. The tavern owner had strung a couple of lines of lanterns which gave off a welcoming glow. All in all it was a pretty setting, one which Slate took in with a sweeping glance as he and Three-Fingered Jones made their way to a clear spot. The guitar player had stopped for a drink and the conversation level dropped to more normal tones.

'OK, *amigo*,' Slate began, 'no more beating around the brush. I want some straight answers to some direct questions, *comprende?*'

Three-Fingered Jones nervously licked at his lips, then nodded. 'Times is hard, reverend,' Jones began saying, digging the point of his boot into the dirt and flicking up little clouds of earth. 'I got me a wife an' a couple of young uns to support. Work's been scratchy of late…'

Slate resignedly pulled out another alazana quoting to Jones, '"Deliver me from the deceitful and unjust man".'

Jones snatched at the coin and quickly put it away then asked, 'That from the Bible?'

'Uh-huh.'

'Got some real fancy stuff in that book.'

Slate ignored the aside and asked, 'Who hired you to bushwhack us?'

He waited as Jones deliberated for a moment and added, 'There'll be no more money, just answer my question.'

Jones drew in a deep breath, then said, 'Remember I said that he struck it rich at them mines?'

Slate nodded. 'Go on.'

''Pears that he put the money into a business in Flower Creek. Now don't ask me what business, I don't know. But word got put around that him an' his partner didn't see eye to eye on certain matters. I don't know what, either, but...'

'Just wait on a minute,' Slate interrupted. 'What's all this got to do with what I asked you?'

'I'll get around to that but first I'm tellin' you some good information that might just help you. Right now I could do with another beer, my throat's kinda dryin' up with all this talkin'.'

Slate considered that Jones had already had enough to drink and was now just running off at the mouth but sighed in resignation. He knew full-well that men like Jones would take their own sweet time and couldn't be rushed. The reverend jerked his head towards the doorway. Before they stepped through Slate noticed that Brandon was leaning up against the outside wall talking animatedly with two dark-haired, heavenly-bosomed *señoritas*. Averting his attention away from his surroundings for one brief moment he missed the trio of men cut across his path, standing in a line to block him and Jones off.

Three-Fingered Jones was a pace behind Slate and saw the men first. He halted, rooted to the spot. His open-mouthed gape and a guttural cry alerted Slate to the danger. He swung his head around and looked at the human barricade.

'Hi ya, fellers,' Slate said easily. 'Wouldn't've guessed we'd meet so soon.'

Billy, Joel and the unnamed white-haired gunsel stood stiff with apprehension. Jackets had been cleared back from holsters and fingertips brushed lightly against wooden gun grips. Their eyes were focused on their targets and Slate knew that they meant business this time around.

Slate's tone was still friendly enough though when he said, 'Well, fellers what can I do for you this time?'

Apparently Billy was still their elected spokesman. 'We aim to finish off what we started.'

'Think you can do it now, do you?'

Billy sneered, anger sparking up his brown eyes. He said, 'Last time you hoodwinked us. Tonight we ain't going to give you a chance.'

Joel said, 'I thought we told you to lay low for a while, Jones?'

'I, I was on my way but *he* stopped me.' He jerked a thumb at Slate.

Billy nodded slowly. He pointed to Slate's gunbelt. 'Glad to see you're wearing that, reverend. Kinda makes this a mite easier.'

Slate did not answer him.

'Gone deaf, old timer?'

The reverend shrugged. 'Something special you want me to hear?'

None of them saw Jim Brandon come away from the wall, pulling out his pistol. He took one of the young *señoritas* by the arm and guided her and her friend to the safety of the bar area, whispering to them not to say a word of what was happening. He returned in time to see the three gunmen spread out a little, making themselves difficult targets for Slate to hit.

As Slate had originally thought from their confrontation in the alley it was Joel who went for his sidearm first. The courtyard erupted into thunderous explosions. Gunsmoke clouded the air and the acrid stench of burnt cordite soon masked the honeysuckle's sweet fragrance.

Even though Joel had outdrawn Slate he was no match for Brandon's readied pistol. The slug from the Colt .45 took half of Joel's face away, throwing him sideways. Blood, gore and shattered bone fragments splashed across Billy's face, making him flinch. Because of that action his aim was redirected and the slug buried itself into Three-Fingered Jones's guts, just above his belt buckle.

The teamster fell onto his backside with a strangled moan of: 'God, no. Oh God, no.'

Slate's revolver was aimed at the white-haired gunsel and their pistols seemed to explode at the same time. Slate felt a blow something akin to a mule kick against his hip and he staggered down to his knees. His stomach lurched, threatening to empty its contents. His own shot and missed its target and screamed away into the night.

Brandon did not know if the remaining upright gunfighter was going to finish Slate off but he wasn't ready to take that kind of chance. He leapt across the few feet that separated him and Billy and bent the Colt's barrel over the man's head. The force was enough to reshape the high-crowned hat he was wearing, and Billy was toppled like a felled redwood. He measured his length on the hard-packed floor, face bouncing once, then was still.

Brandon swung around to face the white-haired gunman, who was standing still, his gun hanging uselessly at his side but still Brandon pushed the muzzle of his Colt into the man's face, yelling for him to drop the pistol. The gunny looked down at his hand gun, his face twisting in horror and threw it away from him in disgust. The gambler spun on his heels to help his downed partner.

EIGHT

Joel lay where he had fallen in a small dark pool of his own blood. His white-haired partner sat with his head cradled in his hands, rocking back and forth moaning softly to himself. Billy was face down in his personal world of oblivion. Three-Fingered Jones was stretched out on his back, face deathly white; both hands were pressed against his wound but still the blood snaked through his fingers.

Brandon finished looking around him and reholstered his Colt. He bent over Slate, mopping at the reverend's forehead with a handkerchief.

'Does it hurt, Joe?' he asked.

'Does a bear shit in the woods?' came the taut reply.

'Yeah, dumb question. Sorry.' Brandon shucked off his jacket and began to roll up his sleeves. 'This is going to hurt like a bitch but I'm gonna have to take a look at the wound to see how bad it is. You ready?'

Slate nodded and looked away as Brandon eased back his jacket. The gambler gave a low whistle.

'That bad, uh?' Slate asked.

'I've seen worse.'

'If it's a hip shot I reckon that I won't be walking again.'

Brandon said, 'It's a hip shot, all right, but miracles happen, don't they?'

'Don't get smart, Jim, it don't become you. Just give me the bad news.'

Brandon drew in a deep breath and said, 'You've got to put your trust in me in this, Joe. The bullet's gone deep, I can see that but I figure if I'm careful enough I can get it out of you.'

'The hell you will!'

'Now keep your britches on. I've done this a time before.'

'Yeah, sure, but did he survive?'

'He? Oh, no, it weren't no he. Well, yeah I guess it was – a big bull that my pa kept. If I remember rightly it was my little sister who shot him. She weren't no more than eight but took this notion into her head that she had to learn to shoot just like her older brother. Mary Ellen was right enough – missed the targets I'd setup and shot the bull in the next field, right in the rump. Took me 'bout a half hour to dig that slug out.'

'This ain't the time to be joshing me.'

Brandon stood up, pushed his hat to the back of his head saying, 'You ain't got the same amount of meat on you as old Banjo – our bull. It won't take that long.' He pulled out his folding knife and bent down by Slate's side. The reverend had no time to protest as Brandon began digging around at the man's side. In no more than five minutes Brandon was standing upright.

'You're the luckiest sonofagun as I've ever known.'

'Quit fooling around, Jim. Just what the hell you talking about?'

Brandon picked up a beer (he didn't care whose it was) and took a swig. 'Your faithful Bible stopped the bullet and you're going to have a bruised hip, is all.' He took another mouthful of refreshing beer, then said, 'You'll be limping around for a bit but you'll be okay soon enough. You're tough as hardtack and luckier than a dog with two peckers!'

He proffered the beer to Slate and the reverend took it, draining it in one go. His forehead had broken out in beads of sweat which he brushed away with his hand.

'For one moment there I really believed

that was it. Off to meet my Maker, you know?'

'Been close to death a couple of times myself, so I know what you're talking about.'

Jones said, 'When you two've stopped gushin' p'raps you can help me out.'

Both men turned to the teamster and saw how much blood he was losing. Brandon turned to one of the card players telling him to fetch a doctor. The man was wise enough to obey the command without question.

Three-Fingered Jones's hands were trying to staunch the flow of blood, but it inched from between his fingers and was forming a dark puddle in his lap. His face was pale and his breathing was coming in short gasps.

'Shit, I'm hurtin' like a damned bitch!' he moaned to Brandon. 'How about a drink, feller?'

The gambler nodded, pushed his way through the mass of onlookers and returned with a quart bottle of Wild Turkey. He pulled the stopper and lifting the bottle to the teamster's lips, carefully dribbled in the whiskey. He allowed him one good mouthful before offering the bottle to Joe Slate.

The crowd that had gathered in the courtyard to see the aftermath of the sudden outburst of violence were still hanging around. It was a fact that bar room brawls and death were nothing new to those who survived on the frontier but there were always those who enjoyed viewing this kind of gruesome spectacle. You only had to see how many gathered to watch a public hanging. Families made a picnic of the day and the youngsters thought no more of that than seeing one of their pet pigs butchered for their next meal.

Brandon felt a sudden wave of animosity towards the onlookers and rounded on them. 'Get the hell outta here!' he yelled, arms flailing excitedly. 'Nothing but a goddamn bunch of sightseers. Go on, *avanzar!* Move along, you damn vultures!'

'If anyone gives the orders around here, it's me, mister.'

Brandon swung around to face the new

voice. He saw an overweight man with a star pinned to his vest standing alongside a smaller man carrying a leather valise.

'Man's been gut-shot, doc. Losing a lot of blood by the looks of it. Can you fix him up?' Brandon pointedly ignored Sheriff Breen's show of authority and addressed the suited man.

'Sheriff?'

'Go ahead, Merriman.' Breen stood his ground and looked around at the bloody tableau. 'Who killed this man?' he demanded pointing at Joel.

'I did,' replied Brandon.

'Head shot, uh? Pretty fancy shootin'.'

'No, not really. I was aiming for his shoulder.'

Breen sucked at a tooth. 'Why?'

'Why?' Brandon repeated, then asked, 'Why was I aiming for his shoulder?'

'No. Why d'you kill him?'

Brandon said, 'Him and his two amigos were fixing on turning my partner into a sieve.'

Sheriff Breen gravely nodded his head. 'I see. No doubt you've got witnesses?'

Brandon nodded to the customers still watching and said, 'Round about a dozen head.'

The busy doctor looked up from his patient, knuckling his tired eyes. 'Sheriff, we've got to get this one to hospital. He's lost a lot of blood and we've got to operate to remove the slug.'

'Uh-huh. Send someone over to get an ambulance and get him over there.' He turned back to Slate fixing him with a crooked-nose grin. 'Meanwhile, if you're fit enough, I want you and your partner to go over to my office and give a statement to my deputy while I rustle up the witnesses' statements here. It looks like a clear cut case of self-defence to me.'

Slate nodded, then said, 'What about these other men?' Meaning Billy and the un-named white haired gunman.

'They're under arrest now and when you've done with your statements you can file charges agin them.' Breen was satisfied that he had covered all the aspects of the shoot-out and considered the matter closed. He turned his back on Brandon and Slate, and made his way into the taverna.

A couple of hours later both men left the sheriff's office and were heading back to their hotel. Brandon supported Slate's weight as the injured man limped painfully along. They were in thoughtful silence until they reached the hotel lobby and they stopped just inside the lobby door. Then, at the same time, they both said, 'What next?' They both laughed and slowly made their way across to the hotel bar.

Slate said, 'The one thing I know is that I need to get off my feet for a spell.'

'Take up a bottle of something to keep you company and rest up,' Brandon replied.

What Brandon said made good sense but why did it seem to Slate as if he was being pushed out of the way? He was quick to be on the defensive.

'You got something in mind, Jim?'

The gambler tugged at the ends of his moustache and shrugged. He waited a moment before replying. 'We still didn't get anything out of Jones, did we?'

Slate agreed. 'You're not thinking of going over to the hospital and seeing him, are you?'

Brandon nodded his head and smiled lazily.

Having seen that Slate was made comfortable in his room with a bottle of Old Crow by his side, Brandon slipped out into the night heading for the hospital.

Perry Willard considered himself to be a patient man but even he was beginning to feel a slight edginess creeping into him. His position behind the deadfall was uncomfortable to put it mildly, and there was a danger of the cramps setting in if he stayed there very much longer. The night was a cold one with hardly a cloud scudding across the star-strewn sky and Willard's clothing was inadequate to protect him from the elements.

It had taken him four hours of stumbling through trees and sliding down loose shale slopes before he spotted the faint light in the distance. He used this as a beacon to guide him on his way. The rest of the journey only afforded sparse cover, brush and a handful of cottonwoods, so he risked himself being caught out in the open on a couple of occasions but his luck was holding out and he made it to this tenacious cover without any alarm.

Willard eased his weight off one elbow and onto the other without losing sight of the house. A neat looking structure surrounded on all sides by a garden and white picket fencing. A horse and buggy with its driver had been outside for the best part of one and a half hours. From where he was Willard couldn't see a stable guessing that it was on the other side of the building. The driver seemed not to feel the need of resting the horse by unhitching him, and contented himself with circular walks around the house.

Willard considered that if the man was a bodyguard, then he was a poor one at that. But Willard wasn't that desperate to attack the man and make off with the buggy. Lord knows who was inside the house; and how his luck was running of late it could have been a convention of bounty hunters for all he knew!

The main door of the house swung open and silhouetted in the glow of soft lantern light a tall, city-suited man stepped out under the stoop and turned to face the woman now framed in the doorway. They spoke in soft voices which didn't quite reach him even though Willard was hidden only some hundred feet away. It was plain enough to see that they knew each other intimately. The man was holding the woman's hand, his face near hers as they undoubtedly were bidding their farewells. Then the kiss: lingering longer than the normal permissible peck on the cheek, and the gentleman caller turned away, placing his hat on top of his head.

Perry Willard watched as the buggy pulled away, as the woman stood in the doorway waving good-bye, and waited until the sounds of creaking traces and hoofbeats were dim in the distance before he eased himself out of his hideout and began to cross the short distance to the house.

The woman was momentarily startled by the knock at the door.

'Good heavens,' she said to herself, 'was there something he had forgotten? Surely not.'

She opened the door to a man dressed no better than a raggedy-assed tramp.

'Who? What?' she stammered.

'Ma'am, I know I look a fearful sight, but I'm in desperate need of help.' Willard put on a hang-dog expression and avoided any eye contact.

'Well, I … I am startled, obviously.' Her momentary unsettlement had passed and she quickly composed herself. She took in his dishevelled appearance at a glance, but his single-rig tied-down holster was well cared for. His face was pale, unnatural for any man from these parts and did she detect a harsher northern drawl? 'Before I allow you entrance into my home I must insist that you hand over your weapon to me.'

'Why surely, ma'am.' If Willard was taken aback by the request he never let it show on his face. He drew out his .45 and handed it over, butt forward, with a smile.

She returned the gesture and stepped to one side to let him in. Willard mumbled his thanks and strode over to the fireplace where a well-fed blaze was throwing out a much welcomed heat. He briskly rubbed his hands together and sighed with delight in being warm once again and out of the slicing wind. The night he spent up in the forest seemed a far away thought now and he became aware that the woman hadn't moved away from the door, and still held his gun in her hand.

He looked at her. 'It's okay, ma'am,' he said nodding at his gun. 'You won't have any use for that.'

She gave him a half-smile. 'I hope not for your sake. I may be a woman, sir, but I assure you that I am capable of using this handgun.'

'Ma'am, I'll not give you any cause I can

assure you.'

There was no malice in his tone and he went back to the business of warming himself. For her part the woman was not taken in by his statement. She flicked open the loading gate, half-cocked the revolver, up-ended it and by turning the cylinder emptied the gun of its bullets.

'There,' she said pocketing the cartridges before handing him back the Colt. 'At least we can set our minds at rest over the matter.'

He re-holstered the dis-armed Colt. 'Yes, ma'am.'

'You look as though you could do with a decent meal inside of you, mister...'

'Will...' He caught himself. 'Wilson, ma'am. Jake Wilson from Montana way.' He stepped away from the fire, his hand extended out to her. She took it and felt his uncalloused fingers brush hers.

For the first time Willard took a real good look at the woman. Her hair was plaited into two ringlets that hung almost down to her shoulders. Hazel eyes, clear and bright, were set in a good looking rounded face. Her clothes were of the expensive kind, the sort she would have to import from Paris, France or London, England.

'You have the advantage of me, ma'am,' he said.

'Alison Rudging – Mister Wilson of Montana way.'

NINE

'Are you sure?'

'I ain't got breath enough to waste, mister.'

Apart from Jim Brandon and Three-Fingered Jones there were only two other men in the hospital ward and they were both asleep. It was close to two in the morning and Jones had been successfully operated on, the bullet removed and his gut patched up. His discomfort had kept him awake but every now and then he could feel the pull of exhaustion tugging at him.

'Now gambler man, iffen that's all you want out o' me, I need some sleep.'

Jim Brandon had wasted no time with Jones. He had pushed his way into the ward ignoring the pleas of the duty night nurse and walked up to his cot. The ashen-faced man was half-awake, looking up at the cracks running along the ceiling trying to figure it out how he came to be in such a mess.

'I'm glad you're awake,' Brandon said.

Jones physically jerked with surprise at Brandon's presence. He looked around at the man and said, 'What d'you want?'

A pitcher of water stood on the stand next to the bed. A chipped cup next to it. Brandon helped himself to the stale water.

'You were going to tell my partner who hired you,' he said after drinking a mouthful of water.

'Listen, why don't you forget all this?' The tone of resignation was heavy in his voice. 'Nobody's gotten anythin' outta this – especially me. So why don't you and the padre ride away?'

Brandon shook his head. 'Things have gone too far for that, Jones.'

'It's not too late. Just saddle up an' ride.'

'Nope. No can do.' He finished his water then continued. 'Are you going to tell me who hired you or not?'

Jones slowly closed his eyes. He was plainly exhausted, the effects of ether and alcohol combining in his blood was making him feel woolly. His mind was sluggish and each thought was becoming more and more difficult to form. His strongest desire was to sleep, and perhaps if he closed his eyes long enough... The gambler prodded him awake.

Brandon leaned over the bed and spoke in a whisper, 'Hey, Jones! You going to give me a name or am I going to have to punch you in the guts?'

Jones turned cold at the very thought. He had suffered enough pain to last him a long whiles yet. He said, 'Alison Rudging.'

Brandon wasn't as surprised as he might have been at the revelation. It was the name that he was expecting to hear. He had that gut feeling about her all along and this visit merely confirmed it. He was eager to hear more but Jones had drifted off to sleep leaving him with more questions unanswered than answered. Brandon thought that at last they were on the right track. Well, at least they had a name. But that left the question – why? What was it that he and Slate had done to Alison Rudging that she had hired gunmen to sort out her problem?

Stepping out onto the sidewalk and into the night air Brandon realised how tired he actually was. Even though it was becoming more and more difficult to marshal his thoughts he gathered together what details he could remember since arriving in Tucson. They didn't amount to much: They'd seen to Butler's funeral arrangements; he'd played cards; they'd spoken to a few people and Joe had seen Father Weller a couple of times.

Well, in his book that didn't add up to a can of beans. There had to be something else, but what? The trouble in the alley had happened after he and Slate had visited Alison and she had given them the cold shoulder. But Slate had insisted on asking more questions about the hauler, his natural curiosity getting the better of him. It seemed that every which way he turned Brandon kept coming back to Butler and Alison.

Brandon had watched her very carefully when Slate broke the news of Butler's death, and there wasn't a flicker of reaction to be had. Time at the gaming tables had taught him about watching people. To see their re-actions of drawing the right cards: the slight-est narrowing of the eyes, an eyebrow raised, the twitch of a smile suddenly killed before the corners of the mouth lifted or the sudden stiffness in posture. All the signs to give a person away but with Alison Rudging there had been nothing. Not one single emotional signal whatsoever. Which meant she was either telling the truth or she was one hell of a card player. But what did she gain from it?

Brandon yawned loudly and figured that it was too late to think straight and that nice, comfortable bed at the hotel was beckoning him. He forgot all about visiting the gunsel.

'Seven dead and four wounded. That's what it has cost us.'

'It's sure a damned high price to pay, I know but we can't give up. Not now. Not after all this bloodshed.'

Bill Skinner's farmhouse kitchen held the impromptu meeting of the Settlers' League. That is, those who felt strong enough to want to continue. The scenes of violence that had occurred at this very place were etched vividly in their memories, and today the bodies were being taken to Tucson in preparation for burying.

The gunfighter had claimed five deaths outright, the other two had died later that day as a result of their wounds. Skinner's eldest boy had fetched a doctor from Tucson and she patched up the remaining wounded the best she could. It was Sean O'Dowd, a sheep farmer, who needed hospital attention but was too sick to move. He was operated on there and then in the grain barn. It was touch and go as to whether he would survive. The .44/40 slug had bounced off his ribs, collapsed one lung and had lodged itself near the pelvic bone. Doctor Stephanie Miller, Tucson's only female doctor and one whose sympathies lay with the League's cause, had left two bottles of laudanum for the sick with the promise to return to check on them and O'Dowd.

Seven men crowded into the kitchen, constantly moving out of Jane Skinner's way as she struggled to provide a breakfast for them all. There was still an hour before dawn and outside it was as black as the bottom of a barrel. Overhead a coal-oil lamp cast its flickering light over the crowded room.

'With Henri gone, Bill we're looking to you to take his place.'

Bill Skinner's thin face registered surprise. 'Well, I don't rightly know, Ken,' he replied slowly.

Ken Pemberton, the Englishman, was insistent. 'You *know* you can do it, Bill. After

Henri you were always the one we looked to. We know we can trust you, that's all there is to it.'

'But what if...'

'No buts, Bill. If we thought otherwise the chaps here wouldn't've asked me to put it to you like this.'

Skinner smiled at Pemberton's Englishness in his phrasing but nodded in agreement. 'Sure, someone has to take the bull by the horns.'

'And you're just the man to do it,' urged Pemberton.

Skinner drank from his coffee mug and waited for the words of thanks to die away. He cleared his throat before standing up. The look on his face quietened those in the room.

'There ain't no other way for me to tell it but straight. When Doc Miller was dealing with the dead gunslinger we went through his pockets to find out who he was.' He brought out a folded length of paper and held it up for everyone to see. 'What this is is a legal document saying that the Jacques' farm had been sold by the Southern Pacific Rail Road to the Tucson Land Leasing Company and then sub-let to Heber Carson. That's the name of the gunslinger who got hisself killed – Heber Carson. But it's only a short sub-let, and when I say short I mean just twenty-four hours. That means that sometime yesterday the lease reverted back to this Tucson company.'

'So it appears that this company,' Ken Pemberton began, taking off his spectacles and polishing them with a crisp white handkerchief, 'is to be held responsible and not the Southern Pacific as we previously had thought.'

'Yeah, that may be so, Ken,' Matthew Skelton said, his mass of dark hair uncombed and face unshaven. 'But who in the hell owns this Tucson Land Leasing Company?'

There was a chorus of yehs and whos. Skinner lifted the mug to his lips and finished off the coffee. He raked his eyes around the kitchen at the men waiting for any kind of answer.

'I figured you'd want to know that. So when I was in town yesterday dealing with the undertaker I went along to see the lawyers the League is using. He found out that the company is fronted by Don Gilburn.'

A few cuss words filled the air, quickly followed by apologies to Jane Skinner. Her husband held up his hands for silence, waited a minute for the talking to die down, then continued.

'Now we know who is actually behind all this we can do something about it,' said Skinner.

'I'll do somethin' about it awright!' Will Hopkins growled, leaning forward across the table. His face and hands were the colour of seasoned leather and to anyone who didn't know him they might've guessed his age at sixty and not the actual thirty-five years he really was. 'Give me three men and I'll ride into town an' lynch the no good bastard!'

Skinner looked in surprise at his fellow rancher and slowly shook his head. 'Don't be a fool Will. That's one way of getting the law agin us if we done a damned fool thing like that!'

'You ain't thinkin' we can sit back and do nothin', uh?' Hopkins' face was flushed with anger.

'There ain't no use in us tackling Gilburn that way. Any chance we have in the courts agin him would disappear faster than a gopher down his hole! No, we have to plan something else. 'Sides, what good would it have done for folks like Mary Jacques, Red Martin's youngsters or Rebecca Ann Lee?' He ticked off a few of the women left widowed, or in the case of Red Martin, children orphaned, on his fingers. 'How would they feel if at the end all they had to show was a few dollars from the S.P.R.R. if we went ahead with your plan?'

Hopkins said, 'I'll allow you all that, Bill, but what do you aim to do about Gilburn? Iffen we go through all them legal wrang-lings it might take weeks, months or even years. Once Gilburn and the railroad start them delayin' tactics there ain't no tellin' how long it'll take to get any sort of justice.'

Charlie Faye, a whipcord thin man with soft blue eyes and a thatch of light brown hair, took up the reins of the argument. 'What foxes me is why the railroad would let Gilburn have those pieces of land in the first place. We all know how greedy the Southern Pacific is – if they can get a dollar more for any section of land, then they'll sell it out from under you. So why are they dealing with Gilburn?'

'Good point, Charlie. And one that needs a lot of thinking about,' Pemberton said drumming his fingers on the kitchen table and looked at some of the bemused faces surrounding him. Only Harry Ayling and Pete Tubberdy had remained silent throughout; perhaps it was proving too much for them to take in at one go.

'Excuse me, gents,' Jane Skinner's soft voice cut in. 'It appears that this would be an ideal time to put your jaws to work around this breakfast.' Her smile was wide and warm.

The men appeared relieved at the welcomed interruption and sat themselves around the large kitchen table. Jane placed two pots of Arbuckles coffee along with a bowl of sugar and a jug of fresh milk at one end of the table, followed by plates of ham, grits and eggs with biscuits. She stepped back to let the men get on with the business of eating silently hoping that there would be enough left over to feed her own family.

Don Gilburn had just walked into his office and sat behind the large mahogany desk when someone knocked timidly on the front door. He sighed heavily and called out, 'Come in.' The door opened and in walked a neatly dressed railroad worker.

'Nathan,' Gilburn said, mildly surprised to see the man so early in the day. 'What can I do for you?'

Nathan stood in front of the desk, a worried frown creasing his otherwise plain countenance. 'Sorry to disturb you so early, Mister Gilburn, but I was keeping an eye out for you this morning. Seeing as I'm the one to open up and take the first messages coming down the wire, I thought I'd better bring this over straight off.' He brought out a torn-off sheet from his pad. Gilburn took it and read it through. He looked up at Nathan.

The man was portly but not big enough to call really fat. His thinning hair was slicked down and parted in the middle. The starched collar and cuffs were a brilliant white and his suit was brushed and well cared for. A man exact in his dress and manners, and more than likely to be efficient to the point of being annoying.

Gilburn said, 'Is this the only copy?'

'Yes, sir.'

'Are you the only one who has seen it?'

Again, 'Yes, sir.'

Gilburn put the telegram down on the desk, looked at it a while longer before saying, 'I don't need to remind you the importance of this, do I Nathan?'

'No sir, Mister Gilburn. When the company says it's secret, it means just that to me. No other soul has seen that telegram and I ain't said a word to no one. I came to you straight off.'

'Well done, Nathan. I can see why the railroad made you their top hand at the station.' He got up and walked around the desk, draped an arm around Nathan's shoulders and gently guided him to the door saying, 'I've got my instructions to follow an' so have you. Let's get them done without all the fuss, eh?'

'Sure thing, Mister Gilburn. You can always rely on Nathan Kelly to do his duty. You bet you can. I've also got instructions not to allow any messages to go out excepting on company business.'

Gilburn gave that some thought, then opened his office door saying, 'OK Nathan, I'll say mornin' to you and let's keep this under our hats, eh?'

He stood in the doorway and watched the middle-aged man swagger away with self-importance, thinking that if Kelly had a tail he'd be shaking it. Looking down Stone

Avenue Gilburn watched the other early risers go about their business. Wagons vied for space as they made their way from store to store before moving on to their final destinations. He raised a hand in recognition to Bob Dyer who owned the gunsmith store opposite. He was just opening up and returned the salute, eager to get to work on the hammer mechanism of an old Confederate LeMat shotgun pistol. Gilburn hung around for a moment or two before returning to his desk to look at the telegram once again. It read:

To Don Gilburn Secret*
WHAT IN GOD'S NAME HAPPENED. STOP. THE WHOLE THING A SHAMBLES. STOP. WE ARE TAKING CONTROL. STOP. SAN FRANCISCO PAPERS BEEN TOLD IT WAS AN ARMED INSURRECTION STOP. TWO OF OUR AGENTS INVOLVED ONE KILLED THE OTHER MISSING. STOP. WIRES DOWN AT THE STATION. STOP. FIND HIM CONTROL SITUATION OR ELSE. ENDS

'Find him ... control situation!' Gilburn

173

snorted. 'Fine when you're sitting on your fat ass thousands of miles away!' He began to tear the telegram into little pieces and made a neat pile in an ashtray. He lit a match and set it to the pyre. Finding Perry Willard was going to be like finding a friendly sidewinder in your bed. Rumour had it that every man, woman and child in the valley were coming to town for the burial of the seven men killed in the debacle at Skinner's farm. No doubt Willard was probably clear out of the country, could have made it to Mexico, who knows?

He slammed his fist down on his desk top. The fat slob of a sheriff hadn't even got the posse he wanted together. Thoughts of Sheriff Breen reminded Gilburn that he ought to do something about him, but what?

Originally, Gilburn had thought he had covered everything but inch by inch it was beginning to unravel and if he weren't careful he'd be finished. There was only one thing for him to do and that was to find out what side of the fence Breen was sitting on.

As far as he knew there was only him, Breen and the two gunnies who knew of his plans, and out of them he knew for definite where to find Breen. Gilburn picked up his low-crowned grey Stetson and put it on. Looking at himself in the mirror that hung above the small filing cabinet he adjusted its angle, then straightened his string tie before leaving the office.

At that precise moment Sheriff Pete Breen was finishing the last drop of coffee and dropped the mug into the wash bucket. His deputy would clean that and the prisoners' dirty plates and mugs when he began his shift at eight. Meanwhile the day started as usual in bringing the roster of prisoners up to date. He rose and took the large, brown leather book from the shelf behind his desk. He selected a pen with a decent nib, dipped it into the ink pot and began:

Date: Aug 22

Prisoner's name: José Chaçon (unconfirmed)

Offence: Drunk and disorderly.

Committed by: Constable Johnson

He left the *penalty* section clear as Chaçon was being taken before Judge Dean later that day by Constable Bob Johnson. Chaçon would probably be fined five dollars and asked to make good to the Red Dog saloon owner. Though it was more likely that the cowboy was broke and would spend three days in the county jail, all at the tax payers' expense, of course.

Breen closed the book, got up and re-placed it on the shelf. He was still standing when Don Gilburn entered the office, back-heeling the door closed after him. Breen turned around.

'Hiddy, Mister Gilburn. What brings you out so early? Want a cup of coffee?'

Gilburn shook his head. 'I'll come straight to the point, Pete. I just received a telegram from the head of the Southern Pacific, and not a good one. They say I've screwed up by hiring those two gunnies to do the dirty work.'

Breen sat down behind his desk and

nodded to the vacant chair opposite him and waited for the businessman to settle.

He said, 'What do they expect of you?'

'What *I* told *you* to do yesterday!'

Breen sat in silence.

Gilburn said, 'I told you to get up a posse and find that Willard feller but you ain't done a damned thing about it!'

Breen leaned across his desk, his fore-finger jabbing towards Gilburn. 'Listen to me,' he said. 'I sent out Bob Johnson and Indian Joe to pick up signs at Bill Skinner's place but there were riders out from the League after Willard straight away, an' *they* lost him. Indian Joe said there were so many tracks half the 'Pache Nation could've slipped through.'

Gilburn jumped up from his chair. 'Shit!'

Breen said, 'If that gunslinger has sense he'd be far away by now.'

Don Gilburn ignored Breen's comment and began to nervously chew on his bottom lip, then started to pace the room.

The sheriff couldn't hide the amusement

in his eyes but kept it from his face. This was the first time that he'd seen the businessman in such a confused state, and he had to admit it, he was enjoying it. He wasn't going to give Gilburn any kind of advice or help; he was happy enough to let the man stew in his own troubles.

Gilburn stopped his pacing as something came to him. He turned to face the sheriff and said slowly, 'If both Willard and Carson had the leases on them, that means that whoever finds 'em could trace it back to me, yeh?'

'Reckon so.'

'I'll let you know that the Southern Pacific are spreading the word to the national papers that both Willard and Carson worked for them and had their lamps blown out by hoodlums who then damaged their lines.'

Breen raised his eyebrows and said, 'You telling me that the Rail Road've taken control of the wires in case someone finds out the truth of what actually happened?'

Gilburn smiled ruefully.

'That'll never stop the newspaper editors from finding out the *real* truth,' Breen continued. 'An' when they do, they'll be hell to pay.'

Gilburn looked kinda downhearted. Was Breen really saying that he would spill the beans – a hidden threat? He figured it was time to reel the sheriff in. 'I guess you're right,' he said. 'I figure that the only people who really know the truth, apart from me an' you, are Willard and Carson.'

'And Carson's dead.'

'Yeh, and what about Willard?'

Breen locked his fingers behind his head and looked up at the ceiling. 'Willard,' he said. 'Forget Willard, he's gone to Texas.'

'Yeh,' Gilburn replied softly, 'but what about you?'

There was a gleam in Breen's eyes. 'What about me? The county pays my wages to keep law and order. I aim to keep my oath of office no matter what.'

Gilburn sighed heavily knowing where Breen was in the play of things.

The room was quiet for a while as both men contemplated the new turns in events. Outside sounds crept into the office competing with the drone of a fly. When the sheriff looked up at Gilburn he was shocked to see the businessman pointing a No.3 Colt Derringer at his head.

'Wha… Hell's name…' Breen stammered.

The .41 drilled a hole in the sheriff's forehead. The force of impact jerked his head back violently. Breen let out a kind of whispered gasp as he died. The bullet lodged itself in his brain and only a small dark hole with a muted flow of blood mixed with cranial fluid dribbling down was evidence of its passage.

Gilburn slipped the derringer back into his vest pocket and moved swiftly around the desk. He arranged the sheriff's upper body to make it look like he was asleep: head nestling in his arms and slumped over his desk.

To him it made sense in killing Breen, but Gilburn reckoned on feeling some kind of revulsion in the deed. He searched his feelings but came up with nothing. In fact, although Breen wasn't the first man he had killed, there'd been those in the Civil War, this was his first cold-blooded kill and he was worried about the emptiness of emotions.

Still, he shrugged and adjusted his hat in his reflection in the window. Looking behind him at the dead man everything appeared to be natural; if you could call murder natural that is, he thought. And casually he walked out of the sheriff's office.

Despite the protests from Jim Brandon, Reverend Slate was determined to get out of bed. Even though he had slept for only five hours the gambler was feeling and looking fresh which was more than you could say about the reverend. Pain from his bruised hip had troubled him throughout the night. Although Doc Merriman had come by, deftly examined him and left a bottle of laudanum, he had taken only a few sips to dull the nagging pain. His hair was sleep-tossed and dark circles were heavy under his eyes. But still he was insistent.

Brandon waited; arms folded across his chest, watching Slate haul himself out of the bed. The man's combinations had seen better days; several rips had been repaired with different coloured threads, giving it a patchwork look. Slate swung his legs over the edge of the bed and stood up. There was a moment of dizziness which quickly passed before he began to dress.

As he slowly pulled on his pants, he said, 'So you were right all along, Jim.'

'Just played a hunch is all.' Brandon replied. He had told Slate of his visit to Three-Fingered Jones and that Alison Rudging *was* the woman they'd been look-ing for all the time.

'I reckon you're used to that,' Slate said. 'Me, I have to take people as I find 'em. She sure had me fooled.'

Brandon said, 'She was too cool. As if she'd already known about Butler before we told her.'

Slate nodded. He fastened up his collar

and donned his sombre jacket, then said, 'What's our next step?'

'Figured that we'd ride out to her place and put this to her face to face.'

Slate pulled on his low-heeled boots with a grunt. 'And find out why she had us marked for death.'

Brandon grinned. 'You sure have a nice way with words, Joe.'

'Eloquent some people say but any way you dress it up she wanted us dead. What I want to know is why.'

After eating a hearty breakfast Brandon and Slate left the hotel to fetch their horses. The grey and Slate's rented blue roan had been well cared for; grain fed, brushed and shoes trimmed. Both animals acted frisky as they walked down the street, their riders having to put them on short reins to control them. After the initial shock of getting in the saddle, Slate shortened his right stirrup to take some of the weight off his hip and settled in for an uncomfortable journey of fifteen or more miles to Alison Rudging's place.

As they turned the corner they saw a large crowd gathered outside the sheriff's office. Drawing level they halted and Slate asked a fringed buckskins-clad old-timer what was happening.

'Some galoot went an' blew the sheriff's head off!'

'Was there a breakout?'

'Naw the prisoners are still locked up.'

'Robbery?'

Old Buckskins shot him a funny look. 'For a sky pilot feller, you sure ask a whole passle of questions.'

'Says in the Bible, "Ask and you shall receive".'

'Ain't got time for all that hokum, feller but I'll answer your question anyhows. 'Pears that one o' the prisoners overhears the sheriff chewing the fat with Don Gilburn. Says he hears this crack, then nothin'. Can't do a blamed thing 'bout it till Amos arrives.'

'Amos?' asked Brandon.

'Say feller, don't you know nothin'? Amos is his deputy.'

'You said Gilburn, uh?' Brandon said thinking about the name. 'Sounds like the city-dressed feller I played cards with.'

'That's him, sonny.' Old Buckskins crackled. 'The man sure likes his game o' cards. Pretty smart at business, too. Heard tell that he owns thousands of miles all round town an' a couple o' blocks inside it to boot.'

'Makes him kinda important,' Brandon said. 'Don't see any reason for him to kill the sheriff, do you?'

The old timer drew a hand across his bristles. 'There're times when you can't fathom out these jaspers. Why I knowed two men who dug claims together for more years than I can remember, an' narry a cross word 'tween 'em. Then along comes this female and *wham,* the next minute they're at each other like spittin' bobcats.'

Brandon lifted his hat and scratched at his head. All this talk of women was driving him loco. He voiced his opinion openly.

'What's that, sonny?' Old Buckskins asked.

'Nothin',' replied Brandon. 'Thinking out loud is all.'

Old Buckskins cocked his head to one side and eyed the gambler, then let loose a deep belly laugh. That rattled Brandon. He said, 'What's so Goddamn' funny?'

'You thinkin' that the sheriff an' Gilburn share the same woman!'

'You've got it wrong, old feller,' Brandon said. 'Just women in general.'

'Huh!' exclaimed Old Buckskins. 'You go an' cross Gilburn and you'll find he's *muy peligroso* – dangerous and mean.'

The grey and the roan shied away, neighing loudly as the undertaker brought the body out into the street. The scent of death made them skittish and both riders fought to control them wheeling around. The old timer touched Brandon on the knee and said, 'Remember what I said 'bout that galoot, sonny.'

'Who?'

'Gilburn o' course!'

Brandon was puzzled. 'I don't savvy. Why should I watch out for him?'

'Damnation! You ain't listened to a word I've said!'

The gambler stiffened in the saddle. There was no way he was going to be spoken to like a *peon,* not by anyone. 'You listen here, old man...' he menaced.

'Calm down, Jim,' Slate advised.

'Yeh Jim, set easy,' Old Buckskins chuckled.

Brandon reined in his fast-rising temper and glared down at the oldster. Age had hunched him over and the weather had beaten-up his face mercilessly. And what hair he had left poked out from beneath his wide-brimmed hat like a busted straw mattress. His light blue eyes glittered with mischievousness as he stared insolently at the gambler.

Then the passing moment of tension was gone.

Deciding to stop needling Brandon the old man said, 'Jim, I reckon you were puttin' two an' two together an' comin' up with six. There's no way Breen would interest

Gilburn's gal – she ain't that type.'

'I wasn't…'

'Nosiree. She's dead set on being rich. That's why Gilburn took to her right off. Him and that cold bitch are made for one another, I'd say.'

Even Slate was getting irritated with Old Buckskins' meandering talk and said, 'What woman are you talking about?'

'Damnation! Don't you know diddly squat?'

'Get on with it!' Slate insisted.

'Why Alison Rudging, o' course!'

Slate and Brandon shared a double-take, their minds flashing the same thought: *That damned woman again!* They spurred their horses away from the sheriff's office without further thanks to Old Buckskins. The old timer stood there, hands on hips and mouthing off a string of cusses at the departing men.

TEN

The hands on his timepiece said it was nine o'clock when Don Gilburn finally reined his tiring mount to a halt. He had stopped in a field of wildflowers of riotous colours which went on for perhaps a mile-and-a-half and Gilburn looked away to the northeast where Alison's house lay by the river. He could see the grove of cottonwoods, her *alameda* as she insisted on calling it, but the building itself was hidden from view.

With the killing of the sheriff behind him, Gilburn decided that there was nothing left for him in Tucson. He'd stuffed the entire contents of his safe into a pair of saddle-bags, grabbed whatever spare clothing he could fit into a burlap sack and got out of town pretty damn quickly.

The first half of his flight had been at

break-neck speed; constantly looking over his shoulder for any pursuers but after six miles or so it was obvious that either no one had yet found the body or that they had no idea he had killed Breen. The broad chested sorrel was all lathered up, any further reckless riding would tire the beast. And if he was chased at any time even this sorrel with its big heart wouldn't have the bottom for further punishment. Gilburn nudged the sorrel into a walk.

A thousand thoughts had flown through his mind as he made his escape but one kept repeating itself. He considered that it was about time he asked Alison to marry him. They had been close for more than a year now and he could easily afford to keep her in the high lifestyle she had chosen to live. Even though her original investments through him had given her financial independence, her appetite for wealth was voracious. Given another year or so he considered that her assets would outstrip his.

But right now a new life in California

seemed mighty appealing. He could have a new home built on the land he owned in San Luis Obispo, and maybe go into partnership with Alison. With their joint acumen they would make a damned good business couple.

But time was running out for him and he knew it wouldn't be long before Amos Parker or Indian Joe would figure things out and come after him. California seemed more and more attractive the more he thought about it. Once she had taken care of everything at this end, Alison would meet him out there and they could start a new life as man and wife.

Gilburn felt more at ease with himself now that he'd sorted out a pathway for his, and Alison's future. He smiled because he was already thinking of them as a couple. He followed the trail that parallelled the river and looked out across Alison's land. The smile froze on his lips when he saw a stranger step out of the barn, walk up to the rear of the house, then let himself in by the kitchen door.

Brandon and Slate headed out of town towards where the railroad was building new stores and a holding depot. They left the modern buildings behind and entered an area of lean-tos and shoddily built adobes mixed with wooden shacks and tents. Brandon shifted in the saddle, uneasy with the area. There was something about it that gave off an aura of menace and it didn't sit well with him.

Slate noticed his discomfort and said, 'Funny, ain't it?'

'What is?'

'That men like me an' you feel threatened by these surroundings.'

'You too, uh?'

Slate nodded. 'I always try and give areas like these a wide loop but every now an' then they can't be avoided. Each and every time I get the same feelin'. Liken I want to keep lookin' over my shoulder the whole time.'

Brandon agreed. 'I got me an itch 'tween my shoulders I can't scratch, an' it's driving me nuts. He shot a glance behind him and looked at the unfamiliar surroundings. In the brightness of daylight he felt a fool to worry about it, but the notion was a persistent one.

When he turned around they were approaching a corral made up of mesquite poles. A handful of men dressed in similar fashion of working boots, corduroy pants, wool shirts and hats were leaning up against the fence smoking and drinking. It was a familiar scene but there was something about it that alerted Brandon to a hidden danger. He looked across to the reverend.

Obviously he had a similar feeling because he had brushed his tailcoats clear of the grips of his .45. The gambler followed his example and raked his eyes around the area. The men at the corral hadn't made any kind of suspicious moves, they still took their drink or smoked their quirlies.

For a moment Brandon was tempted to

turn back and seek out the comfort of the nearest saloon. But knew he wouldn't. For better or for worse he was the reverend's partner, and even though the older man was dandy with a pistol, Brandon knew that in a tight situation even his inexperienced help was relied upon.

They were only five yards away from the corral when a sudden movement from the doorway of a wooden shack to their right alerted them. Sunlight bounced off a head of white hair that was bent over the sights of a Winchester carbine.

Slate was quick.

Before the first lump of lead from the Winchester could be fired at them, Slate had cleared leather and sent a .45 slug at the bushwhacker. He fired again a split second later and the gunman was thrown back against the wall, blood leaking from wounds in his upper chest and stomach. The Winchester had been dropped out of harm's way. He slithered down into an untidy heap, his body twitching spasmodically. But he wasn't dead.

Not yet.

Brandon covered the men by the fence but they had backed away when the gunplay had started, they didn't want to be involved. He and the reverend walked their horses over to the doubled-up body of the white-haired gunny who they instantly recognised as being in cahoots with Joel and Billy.

'Hey, sonny,' Slate said softly. 'Why did you do it?'

The dying man lifted his hand up, face creased up in pain and said, 'You kilt my pard.'

Brandon said, 'Revenge, uh? Look where that's gotten you.'

He swallowed loudly, 'Couldn't let it go without tryin', could I?'

'I've seen men die for less,' Slate said. 'But was it worth it?'

He coughed up some blood. 'Lung's been hit. I'm a gonner.' He coughed again and brought up some more. 'Got to have some pride in this Godforsaken world ain't'cha?

Got no pride – ain't worth livin' is it?'

Brandon ran a hand over his moustache. 'Pride ain't worth dyin' for, though.'

The white-haired hired gun gave Brandon a look of pity, then smiled and quietly passed away. The gambler knew that that look was going to haunt him for the rest of his days.

Alison Rudging was seated near the fireplace reading her book. She looked up when Willard came into the room. He had washed, shaved, combed his hair and dusted off his clothes – trying to make the best of a bad job, she considered. He was still wearing his gun and holster and Alison considered that they were as much a part of him as Shakespeare and his sonnets, therefore she made no comment on it.

She smiled at him. 'Come on in Mister Wilson and have a seat. Care for coffee, it's not long been made?'

'That would be just dandy, ma'am.'

'And some breakfast? I'm sure you could manage some cornmeal biscuits and sowbelly couldn't you?'

Ah, the thought of food made his mouth water. 'It would be appreciated, ma'am,' he said.

Alison stood up, and putting down her copy of William Shakespeare's *Much Ado About Nothing* went into the kitchen. When she came back into the room she was carrying two plates of piping hot biscuits. Her face was red with the heat from the range and putting the plates down on the table she said, 'The sowbelly will be done shortly, just help yourself to these.'

Willard sat himself at the table and attacked the biscuits with great gusto. They were half way through the first plateful when the front door was suddenly thrown open and went crashing against the wall.

Perry Willard acted instinctively. He dropped his hand to the grips of the Colt and hauled out the revolver with lightning reaction. It was pointed at the man in the doorway before Alison could really take in the situation. When she did she said calmly and with authority, 'Mister Wilson, put that weapon away.'

'Who the hell is he?' demanded Gilburn, face dark as a thundercloud.

Alison came over to him and placed a reassuring hand on his forearm saying, 'Don, there's no need to worry…'

'What? I find a stranger in your house, eating breakfast an' lookin' nice an' cozy, an' you're telling me not to worry.'

Alison gave a wry smile. 'Why, I do believe you are jealous, Don dearest.'

Gilburn's face turned red with embarrassment and finally looked away from the man who still pointed the revolver at him. He said, 'Well … well what's a man to think? Tell me that?'

She pushed him into the room, pulling the door gently to behind them. Once inside the men stood opposite each other, squaring off like a pair of pugilists. Alison stepped between them and said to Willard in a tone that brooked no argument.

'Kindly reholster that Colt, Mister Wilson

and let's get this sorted out right now. Don, it's nothing like you think it is. Firstly, Mister Wilson here had been set afoot and I allowed him to rest up in the barn. I fixed him breakfast and in return he was going to harness up Juliet, and then I was going to take him into town where he could conclude his business deal. But Don, you burst in here like a charging buffalo with all sorts of evil notions in your head...'

'Alison, please,' Gilburn interjected.

She held up a hand to silence him. 'Let me finish, Don. Although Mister Wilson has been waving that Colt around like it's loaded we came to an agreement last night.' She dug into her apron pocket and brought out the .45's cartridges, showing them to Gilburn. 'As you can see, it has been disarmed and if you look at his belt all the loops are empty.'

Gilburn nodded and finally allowed his tensed-up body to relax. He stuck out his right hand to Willard. 'My apologies, Mister Wilson,' he said, pumping out a vigorous handshake. 'I tend to get a little over protective when it comes to Alison here.'

'I can understand that, Don,' Willard said easily. 'I would too, in the same position.'

Blowing out a long sigh of relief Alison suggested a fresh cup of coffee for all. Before they sat back down at the table, Gilburn asked Willard to excuse him and Alison and took her through the kitchen, and out into the back yard. Here the businessman explained what had happened to the sheriff and of the deal he had been working on for the Southern Pacific.

Alison listened carefully to all that was said, and gave herself a moment to weigh up the consequences before asking, 'What are your plans, Don?'

'I'd ... I'd like us to be married an' move out to California.'

'Oh,' Alison managed.

Gilburn looked at her, his heart beating like a steamhammer in his chest, and his stomach coiled in tight knots waiting for her reply.

Alison pursed her lips and made him wait a

minute longer before giving her answer. 'I'm sorry Don, but the answer's got to be no.'

He was slack-mouthed with surprise. He never expected Alison to refuse his offer of marriage, not in a coon's age. He managed to say, 'Why not?'

'Given what you've said, I don't intend spending the rest of my days having to look over my shoulder for some revenge-bent settler come to get even for the trouble you've caused.'

'Me? Me? It wasn't me who went out there and began blowing people away...'

'But you put the whole thing in motion, didn't you? You were the instigator; once they find out you were behind it all, then they'll come after you. No matter where you go or what name you chose, they'd be on your trail until they had avenged those murders. It may not be this year or the next but sooner or later they'd ketch up and kill you.

'I don't want to be part of anything like that, Don. My life is settled here in this country, I like it here and I don't want to move. Let's face it, we've had some good times and to some extent we have used each other one way or another. But it's something I don't want to argue about, so let's leave it like it is now. No fuss, no emotional scenes – let's just go our own ways, all right?'

Gilburn could feel the sense of rejection turning into anger simmering inside of him. He pulled away from her and began shouting. 'Listen to me, lady! I've done some things in my time but I never murdered anyone until today. And I done it for you!'

'For me?' Alison was shocked that he would say such a thing. 'Don't give me that! You were protecting your own hide. All someone has to do is to find your name on those deeds and you're finished!'

Gilburn's hands were clenched into fists held fast at his side. His eyes were slits fired with a hatred burning bright in them. 'I hired a couple of guns to do a simple job and they bollixed it up! One of them's dead and the other's far away by now. Breen was the only other person who knew about the deals – he's dead as well. So I'm sorry my dear, but I have to equal things out.'

There was no flicker of emotion from Alison as she watched Gilburn pull out the Colt derringer from his vest pocket and aim it at her face.

The triple click of a Colt .45's hammer being fully cocked sounded loud in the quietness of the backyard.

Gilburn turned his head and looked at Willard standing in the doorway. The businessman didn't know how long the stranger had been there or of how much he had overheard, but he didn't seem to care. Once again the .45 was pointed at him. The businessman wasn't fazed as he slowly shook his head and said, 'Feller, you ain't scaring anyone with that empty gun. Back off, this ain't your affair.'

'If you go by the name of Don Gilburn, then I think it is.'

'Do I know you?' said Gilburn uneasily.

Willard said, 'Not by name but you know of me.'

Gilburn gestured with his empty hand for Willard to carry on. 'What we've got here,' Willard said. 'Is a kind of Mexican standoff. You've got your gun pointed at the lady, an' I've got mine on you. I've got somethin' you want, an' you've got somethin' I need.'

Gilburn licked at his dry lips, thought for a moment then gave a little snort of a laugh. He said, 'Sounds mighty fine, Mister Wilson, if Wilson's your proper handle, excepting that my gun's loaded and yourn ain't.'

Willard nodded slightly. 'You willin' to bet your life on that?'

Don Gilburn hesitated a second or two after that, his mind racing with the idea that maybe Alison had lied to him about the Colt being empty. And if she had, why? No, the idea was too fantastic, he would play his hand as he saw it. He ignored the challenge and took up on the other part of Wilson's statement.

He said, 'You say you've got something of mine – what?'

'First off you owe me two Grand.'

'Jeez, I don't even know you let alone owe you money!'

'Alrighty, let's start by me telling you my name and see if that jogs that faulty memory of yourn. How does Perry Willard set with you?'

Gilburn's eyes narrowed slightly and he gripped the derringer tighter.

'An' Heber Carson,' Willard went on. 'How 'bout him? He was my pard but then again, I guess you know the names don't you? Since you hired us to clear out a couple of them settlers in the valley so's you could take their land an' sell it on at a fat profit to the Southern Pacific.'

'You got them leases on you?' Gilburn said easily, trying to take everything in at once.

Willard shook his head. 'Naw, I've got mine but Heb had his on him when he bought it.'

Alison spoke up. 'Don, that means that the Settlers' League know that you are behind all this, it would have your company name on the lease.'

'I know that!' he barked at her.

Finally Gilburn looked away from Alison and sighed heavily. He looked at Willard before turning on his heels, bringing the derringer around on the gunman.

ELEVEN

Brandon and Slate reached the edge of the wild flowers' field and still had no idea of how the man Slate had just killed in self-defence had gotten out of jail. The only solution they could come up with was that he had never gone to jail in the first place. That meant that either the sheriff or his deputy hadn't done their job properly, but all of that thinking was academic now. The man was dead and the incident at an end.

The one good thing that had come out of all this was that all the would-be bush-whackers were now accounted for. Two of them were dead, one was in hospital and if you included Three-Fingered Jones into the reckoning that was all of them. So both men were more at ease as they approached Alison Rudging's place, and any fear of further gun-play was pushed safely to the back of their minds.

Besides, there was the little matter of the woman herself. Neither man could get over the fact that it was she who had hired the gunnies to frighten them off. What they couldn't work out was what did they know that was enough to get someone to frighten them off? Well, that and other questions were waiting to be answered.

As they entered the cottonwood grove they became aware of the silence. No birds sang their happy, chirping songs, and no insects scampered across their path. Even the gurgling sound of the river seemed muted. It was as though they had entered a petrified forest where everything still grew but all around was dead. Only the clopping of the horses' hooves and the creaking of saddle leather permeated the still air.

Brandon turned to Slate and said softly, 'D'you ever get that feelin' that you're bein' watched?'

'Uh-huh.'

'Got that feelin' now?'

'Kinda.'

The gambler flicked away a blob of sweat hanging from an eyebrow. His throat was dry and he sorely wanted to cough but knew for some reason he shouldn't. He glanced over to the reverend wanting to know what action he should take. Slate was an ex-cavalryman, experienced in warfare and more than able to deal with the unexpected. He'd shown that with the white-haired gunman and a little while ago back around Tombstone way.

Almost as second nature Slate had steered his mount away from Brandon, giving a hidden sniper less easy targets. He was wrapped up in his own thoughts as he strained his ears to pick up any sounds other than those he or Brandon was making. Without it consciously registering he was listening for the tell-tale sounds of a rifle being levered, or a revolver's hammer being cocked. But there was nothing to be heard at all.

His years outside the cavalry had done nothing to diminish his sense of survival. Indeed, his travels across the country caused him to remember quite a few of his skills he had been taught in 'The Sabre Brigade', the unofficial name for Colonel Minty's Union cavalry outfit. Now he was teamed up with someone he considered to be a rookie, and was in the position of having to do the thinking for both of them.

He turned to the gambler and said, 'I don't like this one bit, Jim. It's too damned quiet.'

Brandon agreed. 'You think we're ridin' into a set up?'

The heavy-set man shrugged. 'Can't rightly say.'

Just then a gust of wind moved through the cottonwood branches carrying with it a distinctive smell to the men.

'Burnt cordite,' Slate stated. He reined in

his mount and stepped down to the ground. He drew out his Winchester from its scabbard and said to Brandon, 'I reckon we've missed the gunplay but I ain't aiming on taking any chances. This is what we'll do: I'll go on ahead and take the place from the back; you take a wide loop and come in from the front, OK?'

Brandon ground hobbled the claybank and ran out from the cover of the cottonwoods. The Colt was ready in his right fist as he jumped over the small fence and ran to the front door. He placed a hand on the door handle to steady himself. He was breathing hard and fast, sweat ran down the middle of his back plastering his shirt black against his skin.

He tried to see through the gap in the curtains hanging in the parlour window. He could see into the room: laid out exactly as he remembered it, but there was no one inside. Slowly he began to lift the door latch, easing open the door with care. In a moment he was inside, the gun extended in front of him and moving in an arc to cover the whole of the room. All was quiet. Very quiet. Broken only by the rhythmic ticking of the clock sat upon the mantelpiece. He noticed the plates of biscuits and the untouched coffee. All signs of a meal disturbed. But there were no dead bodies here, no smell of gunpowder – for that he was thankful.

Brandon was halfway up the stairs, conscious of the sound his boots were making on the bare wooden treads when a noise from the kitchen alerted him. He froze in mid-step and slowly pivoted around. His heart was beating fast, blood pounded deafeningly in his ears. He slowly began to descend the stairs, his forefinger tightening around the trigger.

Slate held his breath when the back door creaked. He had seen the drying patch of blood on the floor just outside the doorway. There were two sets of footprints; one leading into the house, the other to the red painted barn along with fresh hoofprints. Seeing as he was nearer to the house and that his hip was giving him some pain he chose to go in by the kitchen door.

He entered the kitchen and immediately saw the skillet with sowbelly in it, the range still hot. He limped through to the parlour and came face to face with Jim Brandon. Both men let out long sighs of tension-filled breath and lowered their firearms.

'There's fresh blood out the back,' Slate said jerking a thumb over his shoulder.

'Any body?'

'Ain't seen one yet.' He looked around the room taking in the half-eaten breakfast. ''Pears someone got disturbed, uh?'

Brandon nodded. 'There's no signs of Alison or Gilburn. The place is quiet and ... say, you don't reckon that he's killed her?'

Slate gave a little shrug. 'Who can say what a desperate man is capable of?' He wiped a hand over his face giving himself a moment to think, then said, 'No, I doubt it, Jim. There's no reasoning behind that. 'Sides, I reckon we'll find 'em in the barn. That's where a set of tracks led off to.'

'That's good, Joe. It means we can stop all this tippy-toeing around.'

They went out into the yard and sauntered over to the barn. Brandon reholstered his Colt and Slate carried the carbine across his body. Both men felt the oppressive pent-up tension lifting. Several yards away from the barn they heard someone moving around inside it, and Brandon hailed the person.

His call was met with silence. The noise then ceased but no one answered. Brandon glanced at Slate and the reverend quizzically raised an eyebrow. The gambler called out again. This time a male voice sang out: 'Hold on, I'm comin'.' Followed by the appearance of a man in shirt sleeves.

Brandon fully expected to see Don Gilburn but the man in front of him was a stranger. Brandon took in his raggedy appearance and especially the tied-down holster. And to the gambler it meant only one thing. More trouble.

'Help you fellers?'

Brandon said, 'Yeh, we're lookin' for

Alison Rudging.'

'She ain't here,' came the sharp reply. 'She lit out for town this mornin'.'

They knew he was lying. They hadn't seen another living soul on the road leading into town. But they did know that Gilburn had come to this place; Slate had followed the tracks very easily.

'Is her man friend here?' Slate asked.

Willard shifted uneasily, then said, 'What's he to do with you?'

Slate shook his head a little and said, 'The whole idea of asking a body a question is to get an answer, not have one asked in reply.' There was an edge to his tone now. 'If Miss Rudging's not about we want to see Gilburn. Now where is he?'

'What kind of reverend goes around carryin' a carbine an' askin' a hell of a lot of questions?'

Slate sucked on a tooth and looked balefully at Willard. The barrel slapped into the reverend's left palm, his right fist working the carbine's lever in a quick, furious action.

And before Willard had time to react, the Winchester was centred on his chest.

'I'm getting annoyed,' Slate hissed between clenched teeth, 'of people not answering a simple question, feller. Now I'm tired, sore and pissed off of being told a whole pack of lies. You want to see the day out? Just answer my questions, savvy?'

Willard wasn't a man who scared easily but there was something about the gun-toting holy man that sent a chill through his body. He didn't trust his voice, so he nodded enthusiastically.

'OK that's good. Where's Gilburn?'

'In the barn,' he struggled to get out.

Slate said, 'Tell him to come out.'

Willard stared back expressionless at Slate. He didn't move. After a couple of heartbeats he said, 'He's not goin' anywheres.'

'Get him!' Slate all but snarled.

'Jeez – he's dead!' he blurted out.

The Winchester wavered slightly but still remained fixed on Willard. Slate was wary. 'He's what?'

'I said he's dead. Iffen you don't believe me come and see for yourself.'

Slate turned to his partner and said, 'I'll keep this weasel covered and you look in the barn.'

Brandon nodded and went into the large building. It was in semi-darkness and stifling hot. The smell of horse piss and stale manure was heavy. It didn't take too long to find the body of the businessman. Obviously they had disturbed the man from finishing off the hasty burial. Gilburn's legs and feet were poking out from beneath a pile of straw heaped on top of him in an empty stall.

The gambler gingerly uncovered the dead man and stepped back from the rising cloud of disturbed flies buzzing angrily now that their meal was being interrupted. Stalks of straw had stuck to the bloodied shirt, and in the rip in the material around about where his heart was. The man's lips were pulled back in a rictus smile, his eyes opened wide as if he had been surprised by death. He was taking that startled look with him to the grave. Brandon's next thought was of Alison. Had he killed her as well?

That was answered for him as he stepped out of the barn. She was standing in the kitchen doorway aiming a long-barrelled shotgun at Joe Slate. He still had the carbine on Gilburn's murderer. Brandon stayed in the shade of the barn, undecided what to do. Should he pull out his gun or would that start a shooting match? He quickly gave up on that idea when Alison broke the silence.

'What are you two doing back here?'

Slate ignored her. 'Is he there, Jim?'

'Yeh, shot through the heart.'

'You killed him, mister?'

'Mister Willard shot him in self-defence,' Alison answered for the gunman.

Slate said, 'That so?'

Willard nodded. 'He was threatening the lady with a little derringer. He made the mistake of aimin' it at me, so I shot him.'

Brandon said, 'Why was you trying to hide him away?'

'I ... I panicked. I didn't know what to do.'

'So you just heaped some straw over him.'
Willard nodded again.

'Hoping that he'd just go away?' Brandon finished.

Willard fought hard to keep his temper. These men didn't know the full story and if he kept calm and played his cards close to his chest then they'd never find out the truth. But, if he let them get under his skin he knew that he'd lose his temper and do something he might regret. His gun was no good now, he'd used the last bullet he hid away in his tobacco holster to kill the businessman, but these characters weren't to know that. They stood there waiting for an answer.

'I shot him because if I hadn't that would have been me in the barn as sure as eggs are eggs.'

Slate looked at Alison and said, 'If that's the truth, then we've got no cause to be pointing guns at each other.'

'It is the truth, reverend.'

Nodding, Slate eased back the hammer and lowered the Winchester. Alison did likewise with the shotgun and rested it against the outside wall. She repeated her earlier and ignored question.

'We really wanted to see you,' Brandon said walking up to her.

'About what?'

'Perhaps it'd be better if we spoke inside,' he suggested. 'I don't know if you want Willard listening to what we have to say.'

She hesitated for a moment before agreeing and went into the kitchen. Slate joined Brandon and the men stopped before following her inside.

'What're we going to do about him?' Brandon asked.

'There's not a hell of a lot we can do, Jim.'

'We can't let him just ride off.'

'What d'you want us to do: hog-tie him?'

Brandon shrugged. 'All this damn fuss over a dead man.'

'Pray that someone cares enough about you when you're dead,' Slate chastised, then turned to Willard and said, 'Reckon that you'll be going to town to report this? Es-

219

pecially when Gilburn was such an important businessman, he's sure to be missed.'

Willard had no such intentions and said
so. He went on to explain what he had
overheard but not of his part in the affair.
When he was finished Brandon was more
confused than before.

He said, 'So what you're saying is that
Gilburn was behind this business with the
Settlers, to steal their land and sell it off to
the railroad, and because the sheriff knew
what was happening Gilburn upped and
killed him?'

'That's about the size of it, yeh.'

'No, that don't set right with me,' Brandon
replied.

'What's wrong with that?' Willard's tone
was sharp.

Brandon said, 'You tell me. Gilburn's obviously well in with the Southern Pacific,
right? He's successful in land deals and
making a heck of a lot of money. But because
a deal gets soured he kills a lawman? No,
most times a sackful of greenbacks would

have dealt with the problem.'

Willard tucked his hands into his pockets and kicked some dirt around. This man with the heavy moustache was right, he thought. Gilburn must have had a good reason to kill the sheriff over this deal and he was only guessing when he thought that maybe the railroad were concerned about the way Gilburn had handled the evictions. And perhaps the men at the top were baying for his blood. If Gilburn couldn't handle that, he might have gone loco. Was that the reason why he pulled the gun on Alison? Any way you looked at it Willard couldn't find a good enough explanation to give these strangers.

He said, 'You know more about him than I do, so I don't rightly know what the answer is to that. I reckon the lady knows more about this than we do.'

Slate shook his head. 'I don't want to get into all this, it's no business of ours. If Gilburn's deals were illegal and other folk got hurt, then justice may have been done.'

'A harsh justice, don't you think, reverend?' Alison Rudging said as she stood in the doorway.

'I agree, ma'am,' Slate replied. 'But things have a way of working themselves out in the long haul.'

'Very philosophical,' she said haughtily.

Slate said, 'The Lord's work is mysterious in its workings.'

'And is it the Lord's work that brings you here again?'

There was a smile. 'I'd like to think so.'

She shifted uneasily.

Slate continued by saying, 'How about we go inside and get out of the sun?' He turned to Willard. 'Sorry, feller, but this has nothing to do with you.'

He wanted it be blunt with no room for argument, and Willard wasn't offended. He said, 'Sure thing, reverend. I'll see to Gilburn – properly this time.'

Slate smiled wryly. 'It'd be appreciated.'

Once inside the parlour Alison sat down and nursed a cooling cup of coffee. Both men declined the invitation to sit down and stood empty-handed opposite her. Jim Brandon was happy enough to let Slate lead-off with the questions.

'Well Miss Rudging, I guess you know why we've come back?'

She nodded. 'You're still digging around for information on that hauler.'

'Yeah, an' we think you know a lot more that you're lettin' on,' Brandon said.

Alison shot him a look that dared him to call her a liar.

Brandon was prepared for her this time around. 'Listen, we know that you and Butler were once married. That you had a son an' things didn't quite work out...'

'How in hell's name did you find out? No one here knows about my past!' Her surprise was complete.

Brandon kept a poker-straight face, pleased that he had rattled the ice-cold woman at last. 'You're wrong,' he said softly. 'We found out from the same feller you hired to scare us off.'

'Jones! That two timing bastard!' She

almost dropped her coffee cup.

Slate jumped in with his questions. 'Why did you lie to us? Surely you knew we'd find out the truth sooner or later?'

Alison slowly put her cup down and folded her hands in her lap. She avoided looking at them for a moment as she gathered herself. Eventually she looked up and said, 'What I did was for a good reason. I don't reckon you'd understand everything, and I am not going to tell you everything. You are right about Cyrus and me. We were married at one time. We met in Denver in the fall of 1870. He was a fine man then; good looking, hard working and *sober*.

'We married a while later and when we found out I was with child we moved out to California like so many others to make our fortunes. It was fine for a while but then things began to go wrong. Cyrus couldn't find work because he had injured himself in a mining accident, then he fell in with a bunch of outlaws. I couldn't cope with it; so we separated. He took Stuart with him and

I hadn't seen either of them until last Christmas. It was then that Cyrus and me literally bumped into each other in Tucson.

'He'd changed a heck of a lot but I recognised him straight off. Ten years had taken a hard toll on him and the man I had once married was nothing more than an old broken-down hauler. We didn't say a word to each other and went our own ways. A couple of days later, on New Year's Eve in fact, he turned up here. He'd been asking around town about me and found out where I lived, and that I was a widow...'

'And rich?' asked Brandon.

'Yes, well I mean no, that didn't come into it.' She got up and walked over to the small bureau and poured herself a small brandy. The men were offered nothing. 'What it all boiled down to in the end was that Cyrus wanted to know if we could get back together. To become a family once again. Stuart was seventeen now and a man in his own rights. I'd last seen him when he was eight years old sitting on the back of a swaybacked mare, his eyes misting up as he and his father rode away into the mountains.'

Slate scratched at his beard, and said, 'And all Butler wanted was to get back together with you?'

'Yes, but as you can see,' she waved an arm around the parlour. 'I was quite well set-up. My second husband was a successful businessman and wasn't one for children, and that suited me fine, and he saw that we had a few luxuries. I reckon that Cyrus thought he had to compete with Clinton, my late husband. He began to visit and brought presents – expensive ones.'

'He'd gone back to his old ways, you mean?' Brandon guessed.

'I suppose so, I never asked,' she replied off-handedly. 'Besides, he was out to woo me back again and what woman doesn't like to be wooed?'

Slate laughed. 'You weren't wooing *him* though, was you? You wanted the attention but there was no chance of his getting you, was there?'

'Reverend, for the last four years of our marriage he made my life hell! There were times when I was afraid for my life from his … his associates. I tried to shield Stuart from what his father did but in the end both of them turned their backs on me!'

'And you've carried this bitterness all these years?'

She shook her head. 'I thought I'd forgotten him, well at least pushed him away to the back of my mind. But when I saw Stuart, how he had grown into a handsome young man, then I *did* feel something for him – for them both.'

'Pity not love, though,' Brandon said.

Alison rounded on him. 'I don't have to account to you for what he did. It wasn't my idea to rob his own partner, was it? It was his. His way of coming up with a lot of ready cash that I could invest in a deal.'

'Charlie Crane was his partner?' Slate queried.

'You did know, didn't you?' she asked uncertainly. 'I mean, Cyrus told you all this when he was dying, didn't he?'

Slate shook his head. 'No, ma'am, he didn't.'

Her mouth fell open to form a perfect 'o'.

'What Cyrus told me was that a woman was behind all this. We had no idea what he was talking about at the time but thanks to your little confession we know now, don't we?'

She stood up and smiled wryly. 'Even in death he has managed to hurt me.'

Brandon walked over to the table and helped himself to a biscuit. Took a bite, then said, 'Because of your greed men have died. Not only your husband and his partner but your own son. He hadn't even begun to live his own life. What chance did your scheming give him, tell me that?'

Alison bent forward and slapped Brandon across the face. 'You bastard! How dare you!'

Brandon's cheek was red-marked with the shape of her fingers. His face hardened when he accused her: 'You wanted more fancy goods, more money, and the only way Butler could meet your demands was to go back thieving. Until he met you he'd brought up a young child, held down reasonable jobs and held his head high in this world. Then you came along and changed all that! He had to compete with your dead husband, Gilburn and God knows who else...'

'Don't make me out to sound like a whore!' she screamed.

'Lady,' Slate said, 'you're worse than Salome and the whore of Babylon rolled into one. No one is safe near you. Innocents have died to appease you.' His voice had risen to pulpit level and his fingers stabbed accusingly in her face.

Alison's face turned ashen white and she dropped the brandy balloon. She watched the glass bounce on the matting and roll into a lazy circle as the tears coursed freely down her face and she began to sob loudly.

Brandon looked embarrassed at Slate, then to Alison. She had buried her face in her hands and her body shook with the sobs that racked through her. The gambler felt confused; not knowing if he should go over and comfort her or leave her to cry. But there was also a feeling of coolness towards her in the pit of his stomach. He just stood there and watched her cry.

Now that the truth was out Slate felt cheated. Whether he had hoped that Alison would have been the cold-hearted bitch she had earlier portrayed or had nothing to do with it didn't seem so important now. If the law found out why Butler robbed and killed his partner they would certainly track Alison down and she would be arrested as an accessory to murder. In Slate's mind there was no way she would survive a jail sentence, so he was left with two choices: One, to turn her over to the law or two, for Brandon and himself to walk away.

Just then Perry Willard stepped into the room his clothes covered with straw dust. He was puzzled by the scene that greeted him. He cleared his throat. 'Er … Mrs Rudging.' He waited for her to look up. 'I've done all that I can with Gilburn's body. I put him in a tarp in one of the empty stalls. If that's OK with you folks, I'd like to be on my way now.'

'Sure thing,' Slate said, 'but you've got to report his death.'

Willard hesitated. 'I wasn't plannin' on goin' into town.'

'How 'bout that unfinished business of yourn?' Brandon asked.

'That? I've dealt with that.' The looks he got from those in the room expected more from him, so he went on: 'Gilburn owed me two Grand, he had it on him so I took it. I didn't take anythin' else, I ain't no thief, you can check them saddlebags iffen you want.'

Alison said, 'I believe you.'

He gave her a sympathetic smile. 'Appreciate it, ma'am,' he said. 'Now, if it's OK with you I'd like to buy his horse from you.'

'Its not mine to sell.'

'I'm afoot an' in need of a horse. I tell you what, I'll give you sixty dollars for him an' the saddle, you can see Gilburn's next-of-kin gets the money.'

'Sure,' she said distractedly.

They stood in the shade of the house as they watched Willard bringing Gilburn's sorrel out of the barn. He had removed the saddle-bags and gunnysack but had kept the bedroll tied to the cantle. The land seemed to have come back to life once more with blue jays winging overhead, and a rabbit bounded into a clearing near the cottonwoods, sniffed the air, then went back into the grove.

The wind had picked up and it blew a loose strand of hair into Alison's eyes. She brushed it away casually and spoke to Slate. 'Have you decided what to do?'

'About what?'

'About me.'

Slate smiled wryly. 'I'm not the law so I haven't the right to choose whether or not you should be held accountable for what Butler did or did not do. I've been wondering why Butler had cause to blame his death on a woman, and all this time we've been chasing our own tails trying to find out. I guess you'd call it obstinance but once I promise to help someone I like to follow it through. It didn't help when you set those gunnies onto us...'

Brandon said, 'If you had been truthful from the start, then maybe a few more people would still be alive today.'

'Don't think I haven't thought about that!'

Brandon stood, irresolute, considering how he could rebuke the woman, but he could think of nothing.

The sound of fast approaching horses broke into the tense silence that filled the yard and everyone turned towards the track leading to town. Four horsemen came cantering out of the grove and halted in the yard.

'Hell's teeth, that's *him!*' Bill Skinner exclaimed.

Perry Willard vaulted into the saddle and yanked the sorrel around. Three more riders came into the yard from the north and blocked his way. Suddenly handguns and carbines cleared leather and were pointing at Willard as he rode around in a circle, desperate to find a way out.

Slate was brusque with the armed men. 'What do you think you are doing?'

'Stay out of this reverend! It's nothing to do with you, and that goes for you two as well!' Charlie Faye shouted his commands.

Realising that there was no escaping from the men of the Settlers' League Willard reined in and sat slump-shouldered in the saddle.

Bill Skinner walked his horse towards the gunfighter. 'Well, well, well, this is unexpected.'

Willard looked insolently at the League's spokesman but said nothing.

Skinner waved his pistol at Willard saying, 'Get off the horse and stand away from it.' Willard followed the instructions. 'Now unbuckle your rig and throw it to me,' Skinner continued and waited for it to be done. There was a smirk on his face as he looked down at the unarmed man. He said, 'Harry, Pete – you tie his hands. Charlie, you an' Matt fetch me a rope with a noose in it.'

'You're not lynching this man!' Slate shouted and moved towards Skinner.

He turned on him. 'Holy man or not – you try an' stop us an' you'll join him. That goes for any of you!'

'Why? What has he done?' Slate insisted.

'Him and his partner killed our friends in cold blood yesterday. They were in cahoots with Gilburn, an' he hired 'em to evict us an' we killed his partner but this one escaped. Now we've got him – he's gonna have to pay for it.'

Slate looked at Willard. 'This true?'

'I ain't no liar!' yelled Skinner.

'Willard,' Slate urged, 'is he right?'

He stood, hands dangling loose at his sides, looking at the reverend. 'Yeh, he is.'

Brandon wiped a hand over his face, then said to Skinner, 'For God's sake man, take him into town, and let him face a fair trial. At least give him that chance.'

Skinner shook his head. He looked at the gambler with eyes filled with singular determination. 'You don't belong around these parts so you don't know what's been goin' on. If the Southern Pacific have anythin' to do with the trial there won't be no justice for us. Willard's gonna face our justice right here an' now.'

The men finished tying Willard's hands behind his back, and Charlie Faye handed Skinner the lariat with a noose fashioned in it. The Leaguer took it from him and weighing it in one hand looked about him for a place to loop it over.

'For pity's sake man,' Slate urged, 'think of the lady – not in front of her.'

It was the only thing that Skinner would concede on and he nodded, then said, 'Take him to the barn.'

Brandon and Slate walked into the cafe banging trail dust from their clothes. The place was empty save one diner and the air was filled with the aroma of fresh coffee. The bare table tops were scrubbed clean, the whole placed looked clean. They sat at a table in the corner and ordered a meal and coffee.

Jim Brandon picked up a discarded paper from the chair next to him and began to flick through the pages. A headline made him stop to read the whole article.

He said, 'Joe, listen to this: "The Southern Pacific Rail Road whose staff were recently killed in a barbarous act by persons unknown were finally successful in evicting four families of settlers in the Santa Cruz basin area. The incident, however, did not go without further violence erupting. Two male settlers were killed as they physically retaliated against the evictions. William Skinner and Kenneth Pemberton were named as the men killed." Well, would you believe it?'

Slate said, 'Yeah, I would.'

'Sounds as if you half-expected it to happen.'

'I did, Jim. I knew that the Southern Pacific wouldn't let things drop so easily.'

'Is that why you didn't try harder to stop Willard being lynched?'

The question disturbed him but he knew that the answer was a simple one. 'Even I wouldn't go up against seven guns. I'm in no hurry to meet my Maker, there's more for me to do down here first. I'll know when my time'll come.'

Brandon was apologetic. 'Sorry, Joe. I didn't mean it to sound that way. I reckon I'll have to mark this one down to experience.'

'Huh-huh. It's all over now, and I hope that Alison Rudging can live with her conscience the rest of her days.'

'I got no doubt about that one, Joe.'

'Still, let's hope that our journey to Yellowstone goes without further incidents.'

The cafe owner turned up then with their food and Brandon put aside the week-old edition of the *Tucson Courier* and laughed. 'The way we're goin' there ain't a snowball's chance in hell of that!'

The publishers hope that this book has given you enjoyable reading. Large Print Books are especially designed to be as easy to see and hold as possible. If you wish a complete list of our books please ask at your local library or write directly to:

Dales Large Print Books
Magna House, Long Preston,
Skipton, North Yorkshire.
BD23 4ND

This Large Print Book, for people
who cannot read normal print,
is published under the auspices of
THE ULVERSCROFT FOUNDATION

... we hope you have enjoyed this book.
Please think for a moment about those
who have worse eyesight than you ...
and are unable to even read or enjoy
Large Print without great difficulty.

You can help them by sending a
donation, large or small, to:

**The Ulverscroft Foundation,
1, The Green, Bradgate Road,
Anstey, Leicestershire LE7 7FU,
England.**
or request a copy of our brochure for
more details.

The Foundation will use all donations
to assist those people who are visually
impaired and need special attention
with medical research, diagnosis
and treatment.

Thank you very much for your help.